THE FAMILY SECRET

KIERSTEN MODGLIN

Cover Design by Kiersten Modglin
Copy Editing by Three Owls Editing
Proofreading by My Brother's Editor
Formatting by Kiersten Modglin

First Print and Electronic Edition: 2023
kierstenmodglinauthor.com

For the friends who have become family...
and the family who remain friends.

CHAPTER ONE

AUSTYN

They're dead.

They're actually...actually dead.

If this wasn't the worst time possible, I might make a joke that they died to avoid finally meeting me. But... yeah, not the right time.

Lowell runs a hand over his jaw, staring off into space with such pain in his eyes it physically hurts me. I want to take it away from him, but I can't. No one can. That's the worst part of grief, isn't it? No one can share it with you. Not really.

"What...what happened?"

He blinks, clearing his throat and staring down at me as if he might've forgotten I'm still standing here. "Um... she...she didn't say."

She is his sister, from what I've gathered. Another relative I've yet to meet.

"There was an accident."

"An accident? Like...a car accident?"

"She didn't say," he repeats, his voice stern.

"Right." My shoulders slump. My first test as a fiancée, and I'm failing miserably. "I'm so sorry, Lowell. What can I do?"

His eyes flick to me, brimming with tears, and he shakes his head. "I don't..." His voice catches. "I'm not ready for this." With that, he leans forward and I barely register what's happening as he falls into my arms. He's collected, not openly sobbing or anything, but I know he wants to. How could he not?

His parents have both just died.

I rub his back as he breathes against me, one hand pressed firmly over his mouth. "It's going to be okay." I try to fill the silence with something, anything, though tears have begun to strangle my own words. "I'm here. We'll get through this."

He pulls back, spinning around and moving away from me. "I just need some space for a minute."

"Of course. Do you want me to send everyone home?" I glance toward the door, the sounds of the New Year's Eve party just outside of it grating at my nerves for the first time.

"No," he says quickly, waving me off. "Just give me a minute to..." He doesn't finish the sentence. "I'll be back."

"Sure." When he disappears, I open a browser window on my phone, not yet ready to face the party outside either. At least I can be useful somehow. I check into flights to San Francisco, noting that there's one that leaves tomorrow morning with a few first-class seats left.

I'll tell him about it when we're together again.

Just then, there's a knock at the door and, when it pops open, my mother eases her head inside. The short, graying bob sways as she eyes me. "Is everything okay? Lowell just walked past... He looked upset."

I swallow. I should tell her. He won't care if I tell her, but I can't bring myself to.

"Everything's fine," I offer gently.

Seeing straight through the lie, she crosses the room toward me with her lips pressed together. She's always been able to read me, but just this once, I wish she wouldn't. It's not a secret, and yet, it doesn't feel like my news to share.

"You've been crying." It's not a question. Her tone is soft, and when she reaches both hands out to hold my arms, I can't stop the tears from falling.

As the first sob comes, I drop my face into my hands. My phone digs into my temple. I don't know why I'm crying. I have no right to. I didn't know my soon-to-be in-laws. I've never met them and have only spoken to them on the phone. But the selfish part of me knows this changes everything. I know that the beautiful, happy life Lowell and I had just hours ago is gone forever. From this moment forward, he'll be a parentless adult. He'll know loss greater than he ever has. And, for that reason, he'll never be the same.

We'll never be the same.

"His parents..." I whisper as my mom draws me into her arms, rubbing my back rhythmically. It makes it all better, somehow. It erases my anxiety like chalk on a chalkboard.

How is she able to do that? Is that what I did for Lowell? Given how quickly he wanted to be away from me, I'd guess not.

"Oh, no." She seems to understand without me needing to say more. When I pull back, her eyes are pinched with pain. "What happened?"

"I'm not sure, he just—"

The door opens and Lowell reappears, his eyes glassy and red-rimmed. He clears his throat as he takes in the two of us standing there, knowing what we're talking about.

"Hi, honey..." I ease toward him.

"I'm okay." He tucks his chin to his chest long enough to sniffle, but quickly regains composure.

"I'll give you two some privacy," Mom says, squeezing Lowell's arm as she moves past us before catching my eye over his shoulder.

When the door shuts, he grimaces. "My sister is already there. I'm going to look into flights for us..." He pauses. "The jet's being serviced, and I don't want to wait. If you don't want to come, or..."

"What are you talking about? Of course I'm coming. Don't be ridiculous."

"You don't enjoy flying." He presses his lips together.

"But I *love* you."

"And you have so much going on with the bakery."

"I'm coming, Lowell," I say firmly, gripping his arms

as I close the space between us. "I wouldn't allow myself to be anywhere else."

He leans down with a sigh of relief, pressing his lips to mine. "Thank you," he says with a breath, barely pulling away from me before his lips graze mine again.

"I was actually already looking into flights." I pull out my phone, still holding on to him with one arm. "There's one at six in the morning or another at noon."

He nods, taking my phone and scrolling through it. Outside, the party has quieted down, and I have no doubts my mom is sending people home. It's what Lowell needs right now, even if he can't admit it.

The moment you find out your parents are dead is no time for a New Year's Eve party.

I press up on my toes and kiss his cheek. "I'm here with you, you know? I know what it's like. I know how you feel."

He swallows. It's not the same, I know. Losing one parent isn't the equivalent of losing two at once, but it's enough. I can't imagine a pain that's worse. Now we're both members of a club no one wants to join.

"I know. I love you." He kisses me back just as his phone buzzes. Pulling it out of his blazer pocket, he shakes his head. "It's Fallon. I need to take this."

I nod, disappointed when he walks out of the room without another word. I know he needs to be with his siblings right now, so of course his sister's call is important, but I wish he'd just talk to me.

Really talk.

From the moment he received the phone call, I could

feel a wall being constructed between us. He's never made me feel like this before. Like I'm on the outside. A nuisance he has to deal with, rather than a fiancée who can help.

Am I just imagining this?

CHAPTER TWO

We land at the airport in San Francisco the next morning to find a car waiting for us. I know I should be used to this sort of treatment by now, but sometimes the privilege still takes me by surprise.

"Good morning, Mr. Bass." The elderly gentleman standing next to the car takes our bags and places them into the trunk before he opens our door. Lowell steps back, unbuttoning his suit jacket as he gestures for me to slide in first.

"Thank you," I tell the man before getting into the car and easing myself toward the opposite window.

Lowell sits next to me, leaning in my direction a bit as the man shuts the door then rushes around to the front of the car.

The driver meets our eyes through the rearview mirror, a sort of apology in his gaze, and Lowell ducks his head, breaking eye contact.

"It's good to see you again, Henry."

"It's good to see you too, Mr. Bass. Very good to see you again. It's nice to have everyone back together." He puts the car into drive as I sink in, snuggling up against Lowell's side.

It's a two-hour drive north to the Bass estate, which is spent mostly in silence. Lowell spends quite a bit of time on his phone, typing out emails and sending texts. It's hard for him to be away from work, even for a day or two. He's not a workaholic or anything like that. He just truly stays busy. I've witnessed firsthand the number of things that pile up when he takes a week off.

I hope it's not stressing him out, but I'm sure it is.

Yet another thing I can't help with.

I slide a hand across his thigh, bringing his attention to me, and he sighs before placing the phone down. His arm slips around my shoulders and he kisses the top of my head.

"Are you nervous?"

"Should I be?" I quirk a brow.

"You haven't met my siblings."

"Yes, but I've met the most formidable Bass child, and he just so happens to love me." I rest my head on his shoulder with a sigh. Truth be told, I am nervous about meeting the rest of the Bass family, but I can't tell that to Lowell. It's the last thing he needs to hear right now.

I'm the one who should be keeping him calm. The only person who can keep his head above water. He once called it my superpower, how I could always bring him back—from stress or anger, and now, I hope, from grief.

"There it is," he whispers once several minutes have

passed, pulling me from my racing thoughts just in time to see a house come into view up ahead.

No.

House isn't the right word for this place.

House is almost an insult.

Mansion.

Castle.

Kingdom, maybe.

Anything but house.

As we round the curve, I see it better. Three stories of white stone and a brilliant, dark-red roof. It looks like something out of this world—out of this time period, at least. Everything is all sharp angles, balconies, and columns.

"It's..." I can't find the words to describe it. "Wow. It's beautiful, Lowell." I lean closer to him and toward the window, trying to get a better look.

He puffs out a humble laugh. "Yeah, well, my parents sure were proud of it."

The driver slows as we pull down the long, paved driveway and around the fountain in front of the house. The yard goes on for miles. They must own acres and acres of land here.

The car comes to a stop, and seconds later, the door opens. Lowell slides out before extending his hand to me.

"Welcome to The Pond," he says.

I look around. "The pond? Where?"

He chuckles. "It's the name of the house."

I forget my fiancé and I come from two different

worlds—one where houses have names and one where they decidedly do not.

I ease out of the car, smoothing my hands over my shirt as Henry retrieves our bags. "Why is it called 'The Pond' if there is no pond?"

He points toward the backyard. "Actually, there is a pond back there, but that's not why we call it 'The Pond.'"

I wait for him to elaborate but realize he's waiting for me to ask, a childish grin on his face. "Why do they call it 'The Pond'?"

He leans down, lowering his voice and answering the question as if it's the punch line of a great joke. "Because...it's full of Bass."

I close my eyes, smiling in spite of myself. "Seriously?"

"One hundred percent." He nudges me playfully as Henry rounds the car with our bags. I reach out to take them, but Lowell pushes my hand down gently.

"Henry will take them up to our room."

"Right." Of course he will. *Silly me, what was I thinking?* I groan internally. It feels strange watching Henry, a man at least double my age, walking away with my bags when I'm perfectly capable of carrying them, but I'm in no position to argue. Besides... I glance up at the house again, taking in its sheer size and complexity. If I were to try to find a room right now, I'd likely end up lost.

Lowell takes my hand, bringing it to his lips and placing a kiss on each of my knuckles. The look he's giving me says he's just as nervous as I feel, but within seconds, it disappears—replaced by a solemn, no-nonsense stare that I recognize well.

He's always been able to do that. To shut everything else out. Turn off all emotions in order to get things done. It's why he's so great at his job. Real estate has no room for emotion. It's all business.

Business requires you to take emotion out of the equation. If I've heard that from him once, I've heard it a thousand times.

We make our way up the long front terrace, complete with a white stone railing and stamped concrete underfoot, and toward the three matching archways that cover the patio. Once on the shaded front porch, we approach the double front doors and he turns the brass knob.

I gasp without volition as we step inside the house. It's every bit as breathtaking as I'd expected. We're standing in an atrium, looking up at three floors and a skylight that bathes the room in a buttery glow. The grand staircase comes down on either side of the room, and directly in the center is a man dressed in a suit. He rushes forward quickly to assist with the door, shutting it behind us as we make our way inside.

"Morning, Mr. Bass."

Lowell nods politely. "Morning. Are my brother and sister here?"

"In the study, sir." He holds a hand out, gesturing to our right.

Lowell takes my hand and leads us straight back past the staircase, where we take a sharp right and turn down a hall. Our footsteps echo through the house, making it all feel very clinical and cold.

A chill runs over me when we reach a solid wood door and pause. Lowell pushes the door open gently, easing his head inside.

"Hey, stranger." I can hear the smile in his voice.

He pulls me inside too, pushing the door open farther, and I can't stop my eyes from traveling up. The only thing I can compare this place to is Belle's library from *Beauty and the Beast*. It's massive, with built-in bookshelves that go up at least two stories and three rolling ladders attached to them at various points throughout the room.

On the right side of the room is an enormous fireplace, keeping the room toasty. There is a wooden executive desk against the wall to my right and a sofa and three leather armchairs near the center of the room.

It's only then that I realize two of the armchairs are occupied.

The woman staring at me with one leg folded over the other, and both hands resting in her lap, is stunning. Her complexion is deeper than Lowell's, a sun-kissed California tan that screams of weekends on the beach or afternoons spent sunbathing outside her beachfront home, and she wears dark eyeshadow, while the rest of her makeup is plain.

Her chestnut-brown hair is pulled back in a low ponytail and she's wearing a simple white dress with black heels. When she stands, her movements are graceful and slow.

She's less of a runway model and more of a portrait.

There's something so elegant about her I find it hard to look away. Tears well in her eyes as she steps forward.

For the first time since our arrival, Lowell releases my hand and moves toward her. She throws her arms around him, resting her head on his shoulder, eyes squeezed shut. "I've missed you."

I feel like I'm intruding on a private moment.

Though Lowell brought me here, I can't help the sudden urge to escape and allow them time together. But where would I go? Would it be weirder if I disappeared out into the hall?

I don't have time to contemplate it for long, as they separate and she rubs her finger under her eyes, somehow not smearing her makeup. "We're being incredibly rude." She sniffles and smiles at me through her tears. "You must be Austyn."

Lowell reaches back, holding out a hand for me to step forward. "Austyn, I want you to meet my sister, Fallon. Fallon, this is Austyn." He sucks in a deep breath. "My fiancée."

"*Fiancée?* You're getting married?" Fallon's eyes widen as she shoots a glance at my hand. The ground has fallen out from under me, a sickening feeling sinking into my gut. *They don't know we're engaged? He hasn't told them? Why wouldn't he tell them?*

"Yes. It's...it's such a pleasure to meet you." I hold out my hand to her, but she hesitates, then pulls me into a hug as big as the one she gave Lowell.

She squeezes me tighter. "Oh, I've always wanted a sister."

The anxiety I felt moments ago washes away at her words, and I can't fight the smile on my lips.

Before I can get too wrapped up in the moment, I hear, "So, you finally managed to fool someone, hmm?"

Fallon pulls away, glancing over her shoulder at the other man in the room. Dallas—I assume—is lounging in another of the armchairs, one leg draped over the side of it, the other foot tapping on the coffee table.

He looks like Lowell, in a way—similar heights and builds; thick, sandy-brown hair; thick, dark brows—but there's something different about his eyes. They're hooded, both in the literal physical sense and also in the sense that he's looking up at us without completely turning his face in our direction.

When he finally turns his head my way, I catch sight of the freckles splattered across his cheeks. The smile on his lips is more of a challenge than a greeting.

Whatever warmth I felt meeting Fallon—whatever peace—is gone now. A chill settles in my body from my toes to my fingertips.

"Brother." Lowell clears his throat, stepping forward to hold out a hand. "Austyn, this is my brother, Dallas. Dallas, Austyn."

Dallas doesn't shake his hand but turns his attention back to me with a sharp upward jerk of his head.

"It's really nice to meet you," I say as Lowell retracts his hand and slips it back inside his pocket.

"Pleasure," he says simply, his dark eyes trailing down

my body and back up. On his tongue, the word is pure sin. Something about the way Lowell's hand twitches on my lower back tells me he knows it, too.

Fallon steps into my line of vision as she makes her way back to the chair she'd been sitting in and sits down. "I can't believe you didn't tell us you're engaged."

"It happened over the summer," Lowell says. "I was planning to tell you in person, but I haven't seen you."

She narrows her eyes at him playfully. "Excuses, excuses." With a sigh, she pats her hands on her thighs. "Well, I guess now that we're all here, we should go over everything."

Lowell nudges me forward, steering me toward the empty chair between him and Fallon, and sits down between me and Dallas.

Fallon lifts her phone from the coffee table and stares at the screen, scrolling through it. "First, I've already called the funeral home. Mom and Dad had their arrangements all laid out, so there wasn't much to do. I wrote their obituary—just one for them both together since I think that's what they would've wanted, given the circumstances—and turned it all in. The funeral's set for this Saturday, the seventh, at one, with the visitation starting at eleven. They'll be buried in the family plot. I think we'll just do a small, private ceremony for the burial, if you're both okay with that. Just us."

She glances up for the first time. "And Austyn, of course. Brent and the girls, too." She checks with Dallas. "I'm assuming you won't be bringing anyone?"

He smirks. "Nah, thought I'd fly solo on this one. The whole funeral thing is kind of a mood killer."

She ignores him, returning her attention to her phone. "So, all that's left is setting up some sort of catering for the visitation."

"Do people cater funerals?" Dallas asks.

"We aren't people, Dallas. We're Bass. And I'm just doing what Mom and Dad wanted. A small party to celebrate their lives with their friends and family." Tears well in her eyes. "Could you not make it more difficult?"

"*I'm* making it more difficult?" He scoffs, touching his chest.

"Yes, you always have to make some smart rema—"

"I'm just asking a question!"

"Guys, come on..." Lowell puts a hand up to ward off the impending argument. "Let's just get through the week, okay?"

"Fine." Fallon huffs. "So, with all of that taken care of, we just have to decide what we want them to be dressed in so I can take the clothes to the funeral home."

"A suit for Dad," Lowell says, wringing his hands together.

"I was thinking of his red tie. The one he always wore at Christmas." Fallon smiles at the memory.

I frown, feeling guilty. Christmas is the one time of year Lowell always returns home. This year, because we were finally engaged, he was planning to bring me with him, but then Mom caught the flu and I couldn't leave her. He stayed home with me, and we were planning to visit his family in the new year, once she was feeling better.

Will he come to resent me for that?

Has he even thought about it yet?

"That sounds nice..." Lowell's voice is soft and wistful. He rubs a hand over his jaw. "And Mom's black dress. The one with the red." He runs his hands over his shoulders, indicating something about the dress that Fallon seems to pick up on.

"Brilliant." She grins. "A perfect match."

"They always were." Lowell's head falls back. I don't miss the way his voice cracked, but no one else acknowledges it, so I resist the urge to comfort him.

"Why don't we just do a whole private ceremony?" Dallas stands, making his way to a drink cart on the far side of the room and pouring himself a glass of amber liquor from a decanter. "What's the point of inviting all of their fake friends, anyway? You know they're just coming to snoop around."

"It's what Mom and Dad wanted. They laid it out specifically in their will. We have to abide by their last wishes." Fallon doesn't say she disagrees with his sentiment.

"Yeah, but"—he spins back around, glass in hand—"I mean, it's not like they'd know, right?"

The siblings exchange a look. I might as well be a fly on a wall here. Practically invisible but able to soak up every word, every tense jaw, everything I suspect they aren't saying.

"Enough." Lowell's voice is gentle but firm. "We

aren't going against their wishes. We'll do the memorial that they wanted, then the burial privately. Fallon's already done most of the work." His tone is dry when he glances at Dallas. "I'm assuming you didn't help."

"You know me all too well." Dallas straightens in his chair. "What about the inheritance?"

"What about it?" Lowell asks. His demeanor has changed now. He's on edge.

Dallas sips his drink loudly. "Well, when do we get it?"

"That's what you're worried about?" Fallon grimaces.

"I'm just asking a question, Fallon. Don't be so touchy."

"It's inappropriate." She shakes her head, returning her gaze to the phone.

"How is it *inappropriate?*"

She stares at him in disbelief, then huffs out a sigh. "Just forget it."

He leans forward a bit, a taunting smile on his lips. "No, tell me, Fallon. Why is it inappropriate? Are you saying you aren't curious? That you haven't thought about it even once?"

"I haven't had time to think about it. Unlike you, I've been busy handling everything."

"Guys, enough..." Lowell tries to ward off the new argument ensuing.

"No, you probably already know the answer, don't you?" He growls. "Both of you."

"Why are you acting like you don't care that *our parents are dead?*" Fallon's next words are a shriek. She stands from her chair, fresh tears in her eyes. "They're *dead,* Dallas. So, if you could, like, pretend to care, at least for a day or two, that would be great."

With that, she storms from the room.

Lowell waits for the door to shut to turn to his brother, who's still grinning smugly, as if that was the exact outcome he was hoping for. "Why can't you just be normal, Dallas?" He rests his head in his hand, massaging his forehead with his forefinger and thumb.

Dallas bats his eyelashes, taking another drink. "That's hurtful, Lowell. I thought you loved me just the way I am?"

Lowell stands from his seat, holding out a hand for me, though he's still talking to his brother. "Don't make this all more difficult than it has to be."

"Wouldn't dream of it." Dallas tips his drink forward, his eyes landing firmly on me. He winks. I look away in a hurry, but I can feel the burn of his stare long after we leave the room.

CHAPTER THREE

There's a knock on the door of the upstairs office, and Lowell answers without looking up from the stack of papers he's going through. "Come in."

A short, middle-aged woman with her graying hair pulled back in a bun appears in the doorway, wearing a loose-fitting pink dress and a white apron. It reminds me of an old-fashioned maid's uniform. She bows her head at him, then me, and speaks softly. "Sir, ma'am, dinner will be ready in ten minutes."

"Thank you," I say, trying to get her to look my way. She turns without another word and leaves the room.

"How many...um, staff members...does your family have?" Lowell gave me a brief tour of the two main floors of the house, introducing me to the staff he was familiar with as we passed. It's busier than a hotel here, with more employees and positions than I thought was possible.

Lowell looks up, holding a piece of paper in each hand. "Uh, I'm not sure, really. You met about half of them today. Henry's been our driver most of my life, but we have a handful of other drivers for his days off or times when multiple people are going to different places. And there's the chef, plus the kitchen staff and the maids. Then the security team. Plus the gardener and landscapers... The house manager, the personal shoppers, our pilot and flight crew..." He pauses. "Do you mean live-in staff or just staff in general?"

I suck in a breath. I've always known the Bass family was very well-off, but Lowell seriously downplayed just how wealthy they are. "Live-in staff? *Who* are you?"

He chuckles, placing the papers down. "The entire third floor is staff quarters, which is why I didn't take you up there. You didn't think Mom and Dad were dusting this place all by themselves, did you?"

"I just...I guess I never realized exactly how much money you came from."

"Does it change things for you?" Something in his voice makes me hesitate and, when I do, he adds, "I don't want you to think of me any differently."

"What do you mean?" I've always known the reason for our long relationship before our engagement was that Lowell wanted to be sure I could handle everything that comes with marrying a Bass. It's the same reason I hadn't met his family yet. He wanted to know I was sure before dealing with the logistics—yes, *logistics* was the word he used—of being brought into the Bass empire. Of course, that entire plan was scrapped and our time line sped up by his parents' sudden deaths.

"It's been a problem in past relationships. The

money, I mean. It's a lot. And not just the money, but everything that comes with it—with being a Bass in general. I understand it's overwhelming when you aren't accustomed to it, but I promise you, it changes nothing. I'm still the same guy who dances around the house too early in the morning and falls asleep every time we watch a movie together."

I let out a breathy laugh. "I'm not going to leave you, if that's what you mean. It's just taking a bit of time to wrap my head around it all, I guess."

"I warned you this place was a lot." His head tilts to the side. "That my family was a lot. You know that's why I've kept you away from them for so long. I wanted to be positive you were ready. I never expected you to meet everyone this way. I wanted to ease you in. I tried so hard to protect you from all of this."

"I know. I mean, I knew your family was rich and that you left to get away from everything, but how you grew up never mattered to me. What mattered was how you treated me. I just...it's weird seeing you here, you know?"

He nods. "I do."

"People have broken up with you in the past over your family?" My brows draw down. It seems silly.

He pinches his lips with his fingers, quiet for a moment. "Yeah, it's...not just because of them. It's this place and the expectations that come with being part of it all. It's why I was hesitant to bring you here. It changes things—people, even. In my experience, people who know about my family do one of two things. They either try to take advantage of it—of me—or they run away from it. The thought of you doing either was enough to..." He pauses. "I couldn't handle it."

"I don't care about the money, Lowell. You know that."

"So, prove it." His mouth lifts with a lopsided grin. "Stay." He stands, moving away from the desk and crossing the room to sit next to me on the office sofa. He leans over, kissing my cheek and then my lips.

"I've no intention of running away," I promise. "Or taking advantage of you."

"Good." He kisses me again. "Although we can discuss you *taking advantage* of me later." His lips hardly move from mine as he says the words, his breath dancing on my skin, desire dripping from his words.

I giggle, relieved to see some semblance of the man I've fallen in love with. When the kiss ends, he leans back on the sofa, pulling me to rest my head on his chest. "I love you, you know that?"

"I love you, too."

"Then we'll figure everything else out."

I slowly run my hands over the cotton of his shirt. "Your parents would be proud of you, you know?"

He presses his cheek to the top of my head, his only response a slight hum.

We sit like that for several moments, his chest rising and falling with my head on top of it. His fingers trail through my hair, and I close my eyes, nearly lulled to sleep.

With my eyes closed, it's easy to pretend things are

normal. That we aren't here. That we're back home on our sofa, binge-watching *The Crown* and sipping on whatever new cocktail Lowell has crafted for us that night.

The silence of the room is interrupted by the sudden vibration of my phone, and I pull away from him with an apologetic look. The name on the screen is possibly the last one I thought I'd see.

"Emily?" Lowell asks, reading it. "Why would she be calling you?"

"I have no idea." I press the button to silence the call.

"Aren't you going to answer?"

I wave him off and shove the phone back into my pocket. "No. She's probably just calling to offer her condolences. I'll call her back later." I ease myself back onto his chest with a yawn. "We should go down and eat dinner. You haven't eaten all day."

"Neither have you." His hands return to stroking my hair, and I close my eyes again.

"I had a snack on the plane."

"Not enough"—a yawn interrupts his words—"of one."

Neither of us says anything for a long while. The only thing that tells me he's still awake is his hand moving through my hair. When it stops, I'm just moments from sleeping myself.

I can't recall exactly when I allowed myself to fall the rest of the way. All I know is that when I open my eyes next, I'm alone.

And I hear screaming.

CHAPTER FOUR

"W*hat the hell are you talking about?"*

The hall is dark as I make my way down it. My pulse roars in my ears, my body stiff and cold from sleeping on the office sofa. I blink and use a finger to adjust my contacts, which have dried to my eyeballs.

"I don't understand why any of this is a surprise," Dallas speaks slowly, his tone apathetic.

"I don't understand why you don't care!" Fallon's voice is nearing hysterics as I round the corner and find them in the sitting room off the foyer.

She's sitting with her back to the window, one hand resting on the arm of the sofa, with a horror-struck expression. Lowell is standing, his back to me, while Dallas sits backward in a wooden chair that belongs to the small desk in the corner.

I linger awkwardly in the doorway, unsure of whether to announce my presence and ask what's going on, or allow them to continue on without realizing I'm here. The inner debate is irrelevant, though. Fallon's eyes flick to me, suddenly aware of my presence, and when they do, every head in the room turns.

"Sweetheart..." Lowell moves toward me. "I didn't realize you were up. Did we wake you?"

"I got cold..." I spit out the half lie without forethought, then rub my arms as I realize how true it is. "Is everything okay?"

He presses his lips together with a sigh. "Everything's fine. We just heard from Mr. Bingham, the family lawyer, and we were...*discussing*"—his eyes dart to his siblings—"a few unexpected updates."

The way he says it causes something to chill in my gut. "Unexpected updates?"

"It's nothing to do with you," Fallon snaps.

"*Enough.*" Lowell puts an arm in front of me, as if to shield my body from the sharp edges of her tone. "Leave her alone. I know you're upset, but you will not talk to my fiancée that way."

"This is family business." Fallon stands. Gone is the warm and welcoming soon-to-be sister-in-law I met only hours ago, replaced by someone unrecognizable in the way she speaks to me, the way she's looking at me. As if I've done something wrong.

Am I still dreaming?

Part of me feels like it.

I hold on to Lowell's arm tighter, tethering myself to reality.

"*She* is *family*." His voice is low and calm, but I can feel him shaking beneath my palm. It's rare to see Lowell letting his emotions get the best of him.

"I can go, Lowell, it's fine." I attempt to leave, but he stops me, his eyes soft and the grip on my arm firm.

"No. You don't need to go. We're discussing the will. Everyone should be here."

"Yes, yes, let's invite the neighbors, shall we? Oh! Maybe Mr. Tuttle would like to join us, too. Someone wake the kitchen staff. We'll discuss it all over a nice dessert." Fallon rolls her eyes with a scoff.

"Drop it, Fal." Dallas adjusts in his seat with a frustrated tone.

Lowell ignores them both, turning his attention to me. "They're just being... Look, it's late and everyone's tired."

"Maybe you should come to bed, then. Talk about this in the morning?"

He seems to weigh the possibility, his head tilting from one side to the other before he nods. "Yeah, that's not a bad idea." He turns back to his siblings. "We'll finish this discussion in the morning."

"Got it, Dad." Dallas mock-salutes him as he stands from his chair, and seconds later, Fallon stands.

"Whatever."

Lowell jerks me out of the way seconds before her shoulder collides with mine.

He rubs his forehead. "I'm sorry about this."

"What sort of unexpected news did you get, Lowell?"

Whatever it is, it can't be worse than I'm imagining: something like there is no money left or they've willed it all to a mistress or a spoiled pet cat.

"Let's talk about it upstairs." He nudges me forward, out of the room and down the hall toward the stairs. Once in our room, he flips on the lights and strips out of his suit.

First comes the tie, which he places on the vanity near the door. He slips out of his suit jacket and hangs it over the chair. As he unbuttons his shirt, I pull my own over my head, lifting my suitcase up onto the bed.

It's lighter than I expected.

"The staff will have already unpacked your things." He reads my thoughts before I've processed them.

"They...unpacked my suitcase?"

He nods, pulling his shirt off and tossing it into a basket waiting at the end of the bed. "Yeah, of course. They'll take care of whatever needs to be ironed and bring it back by morning. The rest will be hanging in the closet or lying in one of the drawers..." He pauses. "Is that okay? I didn't think to tell them you might not like it."

"No, no, it's fine." I rush the words out. In all reality, I'm not sure how I feel about the idea of strangers going through my luggage and sorting my things, but what's done is done. I move toward the dresser and open the drawer, smoothing my hands over the two pajama options I packed and deciding on one.

When I turn back around, Lowell has stripped down to his briefs and is making his way to the bathroom. The buzz of his electric toothbrush breaks through the silence as I change clothes.

In the bathroom, I wash my face and brush my teeth, waiting for him to elaborate on what I overheard downstairs. Minutes later, as we slip into bed, I can wait no longer. I roll over and rest a hand on his chest, snuggling up close to him.

"So?" I kiss his cheek, breathing in the minty scent of his toothpaste and moisturizer. It's a bit like Pavlov's bell to me at this point. One whiff and I'm yawning, my eyes heavy. "What did the lawyer say?"

He sighs, and I realize he was hoping I'd let him forget about it for the night. I almost tell him we can talk in the morning if he'd rather, but before I can open my mouth, he flops onto his side to face me.

"We always thought the will said we were supposed to split everything between the three of us..."

"But it doesn't?"

"Well, it does. Mostly. Mostly, it does. But the business goes to me. I'll be made CEO."

I'm silent during his pregnant pause. It's not like this is a total shock. Fallon runs her fashion line and, from what I know, Dallas has nothing to do with the family business, so of course, the lion's share of the company should go to Lowell, but... "What does that mean? Will you—er, will *we*—have to move to California? Move *here?*"

I have no desire to live here, to leave my home, my business, or my mom behind, but what can I say? This isn't the time.

"Ideally, yes. Technically, if I had to, I could run Bass Industries from anywhere, I guess, but with the headquarters here, it would mean a lot of travel back and forth. I'd be on the jet more than I'd ever be home, and then there's the logistics of where to land it on a consistent basis at home. We'd probably have to buy more acreage...which isn't totally impossible but impractical, maybe. I've been able to work from Nashville easily with my current position. Sticking almost strictly to virtual meetings is easy when you aren't at the top. But, it will be trickier as CEO. There's so much more on my shoulders now." He sucks in a breath, smoothing a hand over my cheek. "I don't know. I haven't decided anything yet."

"Is there even a decision? It's your legacy, Lowell. I know how much it means to you."

"So, you're saying you'd come with me? If I asked you to?"

Tears sting my eyes, knowing he's all *but* asking me to. "I don't really see any other options."

"I could walk away from it all, if that's what you want. Hire a CEO. Run the company from Nashville." He waits for me to say something, and I should. I really, really should. I should tell him that's what I want—that I've worked so hard to build the bakery and don't want to give it up, that Nashville is my home and I never want to leave it, that I can't abandon my mom when I'm all she has—but I'd be awful if I do. Selfish. Cruel. He's just lost the two most important people in his life. How can I take away his legacy, too? His future? I can't think only of myself right now.

After a while, he says, "If this isn't what you want, let

me be clear, Austyn... I'll do whatever you want because *you* are all that I want." His warm lips press into mine, and I melt into his kiss, letting the rest of our problems dissolve for the moment. I know now I'll say nothing. I can't. He'd do anything for me, and I have to do the same. "I love you, you know that?"

"I do," I whisper, running a hand over his side. "I love you, too."

He's quiet for a moment, then rolls onto his back, staring up at the ceiling in contemplation. "Could you imagine yourself living here?"

The question catches me off guard. "In California?"

"Here. In this house..." His voice goes lower, playful even. "*The Pond.*"

I lift up so fast my head smacks into his jaw, and we both wince.

"Ow."

"Oh, shoot. Sorry."

He grins, rubbing it carefully, but waves off my concern. "Just a bump. You didn't answer me."

"I... Are you serious? Why would we live in this house?"

"Because it's ours, if we want it. The house and the company are the two things I don't have to split with my siblings. That's what we were going over with the lawyer. I'm getting less of the inheritance as a compromise for those two things. It...came as a bit of a shock to us all."

"You mean you didn't know?" I won't pretend to understand the Bass family dynamics, but that seems cruel to Dallas and Fallon. Though I'm sure they don't want a hand in the family business, deliberately leaving them out of the family home doesn't feel right.

"Well, I mean, I knew it *should* pass to me, yes. The next in the line of succession for our family is always the eldest child, but there are certain circumstances and stipulations in place that might've made it difficult for it to go to me."

"Like what?"

He opens his mouth, then closes it again. Finally, he says, "Well, The Pond has always been meant to be a family home. Though the priority is for it to go to the eldest child, traditionally, that child is settled down with a family. Fallon has a family. She's been married to Brent for years, so I always thought they might give it to her instead. And Dallas still lives here, so I guess we all thought maybe they'd leave it up to us. Or let us split it. But no, apparently, my parents were very clear to Mr. Bingham that they wanted the house to go to me. It makes sense, I guess."

"In a normal family, sure. A normal home. But you could fit *fifty* families here, Lowell. Why wouldn't they give it to all of you? That must've hurt Fallon's and Dallas's feelings. No wonder they were so upset." As soon as I speak, I regret it. The words come out harshly, and I worry I've offended him.

Still, he goes on without missing a beat. "Well, they'll have plenty of money to buy whatever kind of home they like. Besides, Fallon already has a home. A very nice one about an hour from here on the beach. And I suppose if you don't want to live here, Dallas will be happy to stay, though I dread seeing what he turns the place into."

"You mean you're going to make him leave?" I lift my head slightly to get a better look at his face.

He scowls. "Well, I wouldn't kick him out on the streets or anything. Try not to look so upset. The man's a millionaire, Austyn. But, in all reality, my parents left the house to us for a reason. It really shouldn't come as a shock in hindsight. As the new CEO of Bass Industries, I should be here. Just like my father and my grandfather and so on. Dallas has never been interested in any of that. Not the business or the legacy. This house has been in our family for generations." He pauses, kissing my head. "And it's meant to be preserved for future generations. Our children. Our children's children."

The thought sends betraying warmth through my stomach. I want to feel bad for Dallas, but I don't know him. I don't owe him anything. And really, the idea of having babies with Lowell, of raising them together—in this home or somewhere else—is enough to get me to agree to just about anything.

"Children, hmm?" I whisper with a sigh.

"That's my plan, Mrs. Bass."

"Not Mrs. Bass yet." I squeeze his hand as it sweeps over my body, moving up to cup my cheek. He slides himself down, so we're face-to-face again as he lifts my chin, forcing me to look at him.

"We're going to have to do something about that, aren't we?"

My cheeks heat, and though he can't see it in the

moonlight, I wonder if he can feel it beneath his palms. "Yes, we are."

His lips meet mine again and, at least for the moment, everything else is forgotten.

CHAPTER FIVE

The next morning, Lowell has already gone out for his morning jog when I wake. I freshen up, brush my teeth and wash my face, and change into loungewear before emerging from the bedroom.

Even from the second floor, the warm scent of breakfast hits my nose, making my stomach grumble. I never actually ate dinner last night, and I'm starving. I walk down the hall and toward the stairs, wondering if I'll ever learn my way around this place.

It may as well be a castle, the walls all made of white stone—more museum than house—with large portraits and pieces of art everywhere I look.

Remembering what I can from Lowell's tour, I make my way down one side of the large, winding staircase, wide enough for ten people to walk side by side, and into the foyer.

From there, I follow the voices and the scents,

wondering if this is a breach of protocol or something and if I should wait in the room for Lowell.

That's how this house feels—like I'm going to break a million rules I don't know exist.

In the dining room, there's just one other person waiting for me. Dallas looks fresh from the shower, his hair wet, cheeks red. He's leaning over the counter, scrolling through his phone with a piece of toast in his free hand.

He glances up, quirking a brow as his gaze falls over me. "Rough night?"

Self-consciously, I run a hand through my hair. "Um...no."

"Kidding." He gestures to a barstool. "You hungry?"

"I'm fine," I lie, then wave away his concern, not moving toward the seat.

"I'm not offering to cook for you. And it wasn't really a question. There's already breakfast made, and Pam won't let you skip a meal, trust me."

"Pam?"

He moves around the island and pulls the stool out. "Sit. Pam is the chef. She cooks enough to feed a small army for every meal, and if you don't sit right now, she'll end up making up a place at the dinner table and forcing you to eat. Trust me, I should know." He gives a nostalgic grin. "She's force-fed a hungover me one too many times. Rarely ends pretty. And you strike me as more of a casual breakfast person, so I suggest you sit"—he gestures toward the stool again—"before she comes back in here."

I do as he says and sit down on the barstool.

Just then, a door to our left opens and a short woman with a soft middle and sharp eyes appears. Her brown hair is pulled back from her face in a tight bun. She rests her hands on her hips.

"Well, hello there. It's a pleasure to finally meet you, Miss Murphy. I've heard quite a lot about you." She glances at the empty island in front of me. "Will you be having breakfast, then? I've got a full spread in the kitchen. Anything you could want. Eggs, pancakes, crepes, waffles, bacon, toast, sausage. I can whip up a parfait in no time. Fresh fruit..."

"She's having toast in here with me, Pam," Dallas says, dusting his hands.

She sighs with a playfully annoyed expression. "No one lets me spoil them around here anymore. What happened to the mornings you used to ask me to make you Shrek pancakes with the little bits of whipped cream for his eyes?"

Dallas shakes his head. It's cute, their relationship. Somehow, I pictured it much more hostile. Like the staff would be resentful of waiting on the family hand and foot, but Pam, at least, seems to love Dallas, and he obviously reciprocates the feeling.

"I grew up," Dallas says finally.

"Hmm, could've fooled me." She winks at him, then turns for the door. "I'll be right back with your toast, ma'am."

"Oh, call me Austyn, please."

Her expression brightens. "*Austyn*, then. Anything else I can get ya?"

"Um, eggs sound nice if you've already gone through the trouble of making them."

"Of course, dear. Fried or scrambled? Or both?"

"Scrambled is perfect."

"Be right back." She zips out the door and my eyes find Dallas, who's smirking at me from across the island.

"See, I told ya."

"She seems nice."

"She's nice because you're eating her food. You don't get to work for the Bass family by being nice all the time. She runs a tight ship." He bites off another piece of his toast. "Used to swat my elbows when I put them on the table."

I can't help giggling as I picture it. "So...Shrek pancakes, hmm?"

He shrugs a shoulder before downing the rest of his coffee. "What can I say? I was always a fan of the guy. I guess I related to him in a way."

I can't stop my eyes from wandering the room, confused about how someone like Dallas could ever relate to an ogre ostracized from society.

Seeming to read my thoughts, he says, "You'll understand soon enough."

Before I can ask him to elaborate, or ask how he read my mind, the door swings open again and Pam appears in front of us, a large silver tray in her hand. "I brought you a few extras." She places the tray in front of me and lifts the lid. The plate is filled with toast, a variety of jams and butter, eggs, pancakes, bacon, and a glass of orange juice. "And there's plenty more if this isn't enough."

"Thank you." I take a sip of my juice as she scurries off before turning my attention back to Dallas. "What do you mean I'll understand soon enough?"

"I mean, I get it. I know what you must think of this. Of all of us. It's what everyone else thinks, too."

I clear my throat, hoping my expression doesn't betray me. "What do I think of you, then?"

"You think we're spoiled. Entitled. Too rich for our own good."

"Of course I don't—"

"You don't have to lie. It's true, for the most part, anyway." He shrugs. "But it's not like any of us ever had a choice. It's how we were raised. Our parents were born rich enough that they never had to work a day in their lives, just like their parents and their parents before them. We can't just go to the store like normal people or work normal jobs. Believe me, I've tried. I know people think money solves everything and, don't get me wrong, it makes things a hell of a lot easier, but it's not everything, Austyn. We can't date people without worrying about what they're trying to get from us. Growing up, I couldn't just go out with my friends. I needed security guards and...eventually, people stop wanting to spend time with you. It becomes a hassle."

"So, that's why you're like Shrek?" I spread the butter on my toast, contemplating what he's saying. "You're separated from society based on your upbringing."

"That's why Lowell got away. He moved across the country so he could have a normal college experience.

And he met you. He got the normal life. As much as any of us could ask for, anyway."

"And what about you? Why don't you do the same?"

His brows draw down. "My parents let Lowell leave because they trusted him not to drag the family down. I'm...well, let's just say I've given them reason not to give me the same amount of trust." He finishes the final bit of his toast as I hear a vacuum start upstairs. "See, the whole family is set apart from the rest of the world out of necessity. But I'm set apart from my family. They keep me at arm's length but always close enough to control." His grin is bitter. "That's a whole new type of lonely. *That's* why the Shrek pancakes. Back then, he was the only one who got it."

My throat runs dry, his words weighing on me. I swallow. "Lowell told me about the house. That they left it to him."

He nods and turns to place his plate in the sink behind him. "I wasn't surprised."

"But this is your home. It doesn't seem right."

"This is just a place I live. Don't worry about me." One shoulder rises with an apathetic shrug. "I've always known this was coming once my parents died, I just didn't think it would be so soon."

"Surely you guys could work something out so you can stay here. I mean, Lowell said Fallon already has a home, and so do we. Where will you go?"

He turns back to me slowly, something unreadable in his expression. "You don't want to live here, do you?"

I hesitate. "Lowell thinks it's important that we do."

A soft chuckle releases from his lips. "Of course he does." He leans forward across the island, staring at me. "Did he ask what you wanted?"

"I want...whatever he wants."

His gaze drops to my lips, then back up, a challenge in his eyes. "Somehow, I don't think that's true."

"Well...it is."

"Everything okay in here?" Lowell's voice startles me, and I nearly jump out of my seat in a hurry to pull back from Dallas. Dallas, meanwhile, holds perfectly still, merely turning his head to look at his brother.

Lowell enters the room drenched in sweat, his sweatshirt plastered to him as he drags the back of his sleeve across his forehead. "Morning, sweetheart." He kisses my lips and snags a bit of bacon from my plate. "I thought you'd sleep in. Worried I'd worn you out last night."

The innuendo in his words, and the lie they hold, sends heat to my cheeks and I look down awkwardly. *Why is he implying we had sex when we definitely did not?* "I just woke up."

"I was feeding her while you were out on your little jog." Dallas's words are a sneer.

"*Pam* was feeding her, more like," Lowell says. "And I do my *little* four-mile jog every morning. Keeps me in shape. Keeps my stamina up so I can keep up with my girl." Shame swells in my stomach. He's never acted this way before. Dallas seems to bring out the worst in him. He pats Dallas's stomach as he walks past, though it seems nearly as toned as Lowell's—*not that I've been looking*. "You should try it sometime, brother."

"Hey, Lowell?" Dallas asks, sounding sincere.

"Yeah?"

"Do me a favor?"

"What's that?"

"If I ever start needing to run to keep up with my girl, just shoot me, okay?"

Lowell rolls his eyes. "Speaking of *my* girl, what were you two talking about?"

"Nothing really," Dallas answers before I can. "I was just telling Austyn how much will change for her once she's in this house. Once she's officially *the* Mrs. Bass."

"Nothing will change," Lowell says quickly. "Ignore him."

I pick at my food, my appetite suddenly lost. "We were talking about what it will look like if we move in. And...where he would go."

Lowell pulls a bottle of water from the fridge. "I don't want you worrying about that, okay? Dallas will be fine. Won't you, brother?"

"Fine and dandy" comes the reply. With that, Dallas helps himself to a corner piece of toast from my plate and leaves the room. When he's gone, Lowell smiles at me over the counter. Suddenly, the massive Bass mansion is starting to feel very small.

CHAPTER SIX

I run my hands over my black dress as I slip out of the car. Beside me, Lowell adjusts his dark sunglasses, trying to avoid eye contact as he swipes away a tear.

It's been a hard morning. No matter how well prepared he thought he was for the day we would say goodbye to his parents, no one can ever truly be ready for the stunning realization that it's actually happening.

His fingers lace with mine—hands trembling—as we make our way toward the back of the house. It's foggy, a cool mist settling in, and the sun hasn't made an appearance yet. The scene ahead of me is nearly ominous, the trees and plants all dead, the sky as gray as mountain rock. Prowling clouds overhead warn of an impending storm.

Just ahead, I can make out the silhouette of Fallon, her husband Brent, and their young daughters, Harriet and Harmony. Harmony, who looks to be around a year old, is cautious on her feet, still stumbling as she learns to walk, while her older sister holds her hand and gently guides her. I'd guess Harriet is about eight, though you'd never know it from her patient, obedient demeanor. Lagging behind us is Dallas, who's been sipping from his flask all day and, as far as I can tell, hasn't said a word to anyone.

The cemetery is larger than I expected, with every member of the Bass family coming to rest on these grounds. Nearby, I spy the gardener's tool shed and farther back, I can see the pond Lowell mentioned.

It's peaceful and stoic and cold.

The world around us feels empty. Forever changed by what we're about to do.

The caskets are already in the ground, per the Bass parents' request, so we stop to gather around the large grave, staring down into the dark depths.

After a few minutes pass, Brent bends down to scoop up Harmony, placing her on his hip. No longer responsible for her younger sister, Harriet leans into her mother's side, her shoulders shaking with silent sobs.

This is the moment I've been waiting for, I realize. When all the walls come down, the masks slide off, and I can finally see my new family for what they are.

Now, more than ever, I understand why Fallon pushed so hard for a private burial. For a moment of seclusion among the chaos the funeral brought.

For the first time all day, perhaps all week, I see the facade washing away.

Cool mist dots my cheeks, and in the distance, I see the staff moving around to encircle us. A few of them—

groundskeepers, I realize—are carrying shovels, their faces downtrodden, shoulders slumped. I spot Pam, who offers me a reassuring, lopsided grin.

The staff is close enough to provide comfort yet far enough away to make it obvious they aren't a part of the immediate family. It's an odd sort of disconnect.

"Go on," Fallon whispers, nudging her older daughter forward. She bends at her knees, the edges of her black dress dusting the wet ground, and gathers a handful of dirt in her palm. Somehow, I know it's the Bass blood in her that refuses to let her look back, to show any sign of uncertainty, as she squares her shoulders and tosses the dirt into the hole.

The rest of the family follows suit, Harmony next—still unsteady on her little feet—with the help of her father, then Lowell, Fallon, and Dallas. Once they're done, the groundskeepers approach, making quick work to begin shoveling the loose dirt from its pile into the ground. I glance around, reading the names and dates on the other headstones in the family plot.

Years and years of Bass family members, years and years of stories.

Tears fill my eyes as I flash forward to a day when Lowell's body will be lowered into this earth, mine next to him. The ground I'm standing on could very well be my final resting place.

Lowell's hand slides across my back, coming to rest in the center. He draws me into his side, and I slip my arm around him. These are the moments I signed up for when

I agreed to be his wife. The sacrifices, the unconditional love and support.

And yet, ever since the moment we learned of their deaths, I can't shake the feeling that I'm somehow failing him.

Everything happened so suddenly I can't help thinking there's more he needs from me, more I'm unable to give him.

A drop of rain hits my cheek, heavier than the mist earlier, and Brent lifts an umbrella to cover Fallon's head. Lowell turns us away, though I meet his eyes, planning to tell him I'll stand in the rain all day if that's what he needs when I feel the rain stop. I glance up at the umbrella sheltering me, then check over my shoulder where Dallas stands.

He scowls. "Don't look at me like that. This isn't a thing. Just take the umbrella." He passes it to his brother just as the rain begins to downpour.

I duck down, the sound of the rain slapping onto the umbrella drowning out everything else. "Thank you!" I shout, but he's already walking away.

Lowell urges me forward, steering us toward the house. "Come on."

The Bass family home—*The Pond*—sits on what must be hundreds of acres, surrounded by forest in every direction. There's at least a two-acre distance between the cemetery and the house, but we make it in no time, all soaked to the bone despite our attempts to stay covered with the umbrellas.

The girls remove their coats and kick their muddy

boots off, carefully placing them next to the door before Fallon and Brent whisk them into the kitchen.

"We'll see if someone's around to whip us up some hot chocolate," Fallon promises. "What do you say?"

I drape my long, black peacoat over one arm, running a hand through my hair as Lowell and Dallas remove their own shoes and hang up their coats.

"We should talk," Lowell says when Dallas goes to walk away.

His eyes dart to me, then back to Lowell. "About?"

"Let's go into the study." He holds an arm out, gesturing for us both to lead the way.

In the study, Dallas takes a seat while Lowell turns the dial to start the gas fireplace. Realizing I'm still holding my coat, I drape it over a hook on the wall and join Lowell near the desk. "Everything okay?"

He looks at Dallas. "I didn't want to bring it up this morning, but I was talking to Mr. Bingham at the funeral and he had some rather...er, *unfortunate* news."

"Unfortunate like our parents dying? Hate to break it to you,"—Dallas winces, his head cocked to the side—"but I already know."

Lowell ignores the comment. "Apparently, the will can't be carried out yet because the investigation is still ongoing."

"What investigation?" My question draws their attention to me as Dallas straightens in his chair.

"It's nothing for you to worry about, sweetheart—" Lowell says.

At the same time, Dallas says, "Wait. You didn't tell her?" His eyes bulge.

Lowell groans.

"Tell me what?"

"Why would you bring her in here if you weren't going to tell her?" Dallas asks, almost as if he is enjoying the tension.

"It's not that I was trying *not* to tell you. I've just had so much on my plate. I don't want you to worry, though. We're getting it all straightened out." Lowell eases down on the edge of the desk, clasping his hands together. "Apparently, the police are still considering our parents' deaths *suspicious*. And until they close the case, we're all just sort of in limbo."

"Suspicious how? I thought you said your parents died in an accident?"

Dallas scoffs, his eyes widening even more as he stares at his brother. "Well, isn't this a sticky situation?"

"It was an—" He puts out a hand to stop Dallas's interruption. "It *was* an accident, just not the kind you were thinking of. I'm sorry for not being completely up front with you. I've just been trying to work it all out in my head, and, I have to admit, it doesn't totally make sense, but..." He drops his head with a sigh. "Our parents died of an overdose." He winces when he looks up at me. "And see, that's exactly why I didn't want to tell you like this. Because I get it. I know what you must be thinking. I know the sort of judgments that come with that sort of thing. But my parents weren't addicts. They just liked to..."

"Get high?" Dallas offers.

Lowell rolls his eyes. "They liked to have a good time. Drinks, drugs—coke, mostly, but an occasional—"

"Or not so occasional," Dallas interrupts.

Lowell cuts a hard glance his way."*—mix of other things.* Anyway, their doctors had told them to cut back. They were getting older, and they couldn't handle what they used to. Dad had a stroke a few years ago, but they... thought they were invincible." He shakes his head.

"What's going on in here?" Fallon appears in the doorway, her dark hair frizzing near her face from the rain. "Why the hell are you meeting without me?"

"Oh, Jesus. Breathe, Fal. If it was a top-secret meeting, don't ya think we'd have found a better hiding spot than the study with the door standing wide open?" Dallas scowls. "*Bad News Bears* here is telling us we're not getting any money until they figure out what happened to Mom and Dad."

"*What happened?*" She steps forward into the room. "What do you mean *what* happened? We know what happened to them." She looks at Lowell with utter confusion. "Don't we?"

"Yes, of course we do. It's a formality. I didn't want to talk about it in front of the kids, which is why I didn't call you in here, but Bingham said it could still be a few more days, maybe even a few more weeks. I was just giving Dallas a heads-up."

"A few more weeks? Well, that's ridiculous." She groans. "Can't you do something about it?"

"Yeah, now that I know it's an issue, I'm going to call

in a favor with Dad's guy down at the station. What's his name? Rupert? Ronald?"

"Tom," Dallas answers. "It's Tom."

"Oh, right. Tom. Okay, well, I'm going to call Tom and see if he can get the case closed sooner, but—"

"But, wait, don't you all want to know the truth?" The words escape my mouth before I'm ready for them to. Every eye in the room falls to me. "I mean, *if* the police think something happened to your parents, they must have some reason behind it. Don't you want to know if..." I can't bring myself to say the words. They sound ridiculous, even in my mind.

"Something *did* happen to our parents, Austyn," Fallon sneers, her upper lip curling. "They died, in case you hadn't noticed."

Lowell steps between us. "Look, it's just a formality because of the circumstances of their deaths. Anything involving drugs means they need to take a deeper look, but we know our parents. And we're all just ready to get this taken care of so we can move on." He bounces his hand in the air, trying to keep me calm. "I understand what you're saying, but trust me, there's nothing to find. It was an accident. And when it comes to our family, there's no lack of things the media will drag up for a juicy story. So, if they get word of this, it'll be a fiasco. The best thing for *all of us*,"—he stresses the words—"is that the police put this all to bed as soon as possible."

I want to argue, to tell him this doesn't feel right, but I'm clearly outnumbered. "Okay," I say finally, wanting to fold myself up and disappear. I don't know why I always feel so small around them. So insignificant. It's my problem, not theirs, but it's frustrating, nonetheless.

"So, we're good?" Fallon asks, hand outstretched in the air as she looks at Lowell, wiggling a finger between them, like they're the only two in the room. "You're handling this?"

"I am, yeah," he vows. "Actually, I should go make the call now. Austyn, why don't you go change into dry clothes before we eat?"

And, like the obedient little puppet I'm starting to feel like, I nod and stand, leaving the room without a word.

CHAPTER SEVEN

We're in the middle of dinner when my phone buzzes inside my pocket. At first, I assume it's an email or social media notification, so I plan to ignore it. When it buzzes again, I realize someone must be calling me and reach into my pocket.

No one calls me except for Mom, and she wouldn't be calling unless it's an emergency. She knows today was the funeral and that I need to be available for Lowell whenever he needs me.

When I glance down at the screen, confusion washes over me, then a memory flashes in my mind.

Why is Emily calling me again?

I meant to call her back after I missed her call before, but it had honestly slipped my mind. Besides, I assumed it was likely just a sympathy call after she'd heard the news about Lowell's parents.

I haven't heard from her in what feels like forever.

"Everything okay?" Lowell is staring at me from

across the table with a wary expression. "Do you need to take that?"

"Sorry." I consider ignoring it again, but something tells me not to. "Yeah, I probably should. I'll be right back."

He nods, taking a sip of his wine as I stand from the table. I exit the dining room, pass through the kitchen, the foyer, and make my way into a small sitting room.

I've already missed her call, so I sink down onto the sofa and tap her name in my call log.

"Hey, stranger." Her voice is like medicine I didn't realize I needed. It sounds just like I remembered. Soft and raspy and ever so calm.

"Hey, Em. I'm sorry I didn't get to the phone in time. I saw you'd called before, but things have been crazy around here. I haven't had a chance to call you back."

"Of course. I'm sorry to be bothering you when I know you're going through so much. I heard about Lowell's parents. I'm so sorry for your loss. It must be devastating for you guys. Especially after everything with your dad."

I pat my chest, trying to distract myself from the tears that come at the mere mention of him. "Thanks. It means a lot that you called. We're doing okay. It's been a... trying...few days, but we'll get through it together."

"Of course you will. I never doubted it." She hums softly to herself, a calming, audible breath. "Listen, I know it's terrible timing, but I wondered if I could ask when you think you'll be back home?"

"Home? As in Nashville?"

"You're still living there, aren't you?"

"Um, well, yes, we are." I pause, trying to quickly decide why she's asking and what might be an accurate answer. "To be honest, I'm not sure when we'll be back. There are things Lowell has to deal with here with his family, and it might be a while. I can let you know when we have things more worked out. Will you be in town? Were you wanting to get together?" My fingers trace the seam of the sofa.

"Of course. Of course." She sounds almost as if she's angry with herself. "I should've realized. It's so insensitive of me to call right now. You must be in the middle of so much."

"No," I lie, "you're fine. Honestly. I appreciate your call. It's been so long."

"It has." Her words are a sigh. "Which makes the reason for my call seem that much worse."

"What do you mean?"

"Well, I was sort of hoping I might stay with you for a few days."

"S-stay with me?" Her question throws me for a loop. Whatever I'd been expecting, this isn't it. "What do you mean?"

When she speaks again, there's no power behind her voice. "Grayson and I are getting a divorce."

"What?" My gasp is a thousand percent genuine as I lean back onto the sofa with horror. Emily and her husband have been together since we were all in college. I was the maid of honor at their wedding. Try as I might to reckon with what she's said, I can't bring myself to accept it. I remember the way he looked at her. The way his eyes lit up when she entered the room, not just on their wedding day but on a random Tuesday when we were all studying in the library or at a party we would pretend not to care about. Though we haven't spoken in over a year—*is it two years by now?*—I see their frequent social media updates. If there was ever a golden couple, a couple I'd swear the sun rose and set with, it would be Emily and Grayson.

"It's been coming for a while, I think. He's been distant lately. At first I thought he was just busy with work, but...I don't know. Maybe I just didn't want to see the writing on the wall. And I feel so shitty calling you and dumping all of this on your plate when you clearly have enough to deal with, but...you were the first person I thought of."

Heat blooms in my chest at her words. So much has changed since we last spoke, and yet, nothing at all has changed.

"I have other friends, of course, but you get it, you know? You knew us better than anyone. I'm sorry I haven't been in touch as much as I should've this past year."

"No, don't. We've both been busy. You don't have to apologize for that."

I think back over the last year. She and Grayson were in Santorini during the summer. Palma de Mallorca in late spring. They'd gone to Toronto at some point...or was that the year before? Either way, they are free spirited and fun. I imagine they were rather bored with the quiet life Lowell and I have built.

No jet-setting to Paris, no weekend getaways to Bora Bora.

Not that we aren't able to afford it, obviously. But our work schedules are too demanding. I have the bakery to look after, and though I trust my employees, the idea of stepping away from it for weeks on end gives me hives. It's my baby. The only thing I've ever completely owned myself. And Lowell's connection to Bass Industries is different, of course, but no less demanding.

Still, as much as I love our life, I can't deny the pangs of jealousy I'd occasionally felt over seeing the latest update from Emily and Grayson. They'd always seemed so...perfect. Happy. Something. Everything.

Was it all a big charade for social media? Lowell and I were never big on posting about our relationship on social media, but now I realize ours may have been the strongest relationship of the two, after all.

What am I doing?

Guilt weighs on me. I'm being a terrible friend. She's trusting me with this big, scary life event, and here I am practically celebrating the demise of her marriage.

"Anyway, he brought it up a few weeks ago, but I thought it was just in the heat of an argument. Then, last week, he told me I should get a lawyer."

"I'm so sorry, Emily."

"Thanks." She sniffles. "I'll be okay. I mean, we don't have kids or anything, and we pretty much agree on what we'll split and who'll take what. So, things could be worse."

"That doesn't make any of this okay. I just can't believe it."

"Me either, honestly. I'm still processing everything, which is why I was hoping to get away from the house for a while. But I don't want to go to a hotel alone. I'll just drink, and that's the last thing I need right now. I'm three months sober." She scoffs. "Maybe that's why he's leaving me. I'm not the life of the party I once was."

"I'm sure that's not true." I shake my head, trying to think. "And if it is, shame on him. That says more about him than it does you."

"Thanks." Her voice is soft. "Anyway, I'm sorry to have bothered you. Could you just...maybe you could call me when you're back in town? Even if staying with you isn't an option, I'd love to catch up."

"Yeah, of course. I'm really sorry I'm not home. I feel so terrible."

"Don't be silly. It's just bad timing. I'll figure it out." She sniffles, worsening my guilt. An offer I can't commit to balances on my tongue. "I'm a big girl."

"I mean, I can't guarantee I can make it happen, but maybe I could check with Lowell to see if he'd mind me coming home a bit earlier than he does. He'll still have to stay awhile to deal with...everything, but maybe he wouldn't mind if I came back to see you." I wince as I say the words. Either way, I'm going to be letting someone down. Emily should be the obvious choice. She's a friend I haven't spoken to in over a year. But that doesn't erase our history. It doesn't erase all we've been through together, all the times she's been there when I needed her. The first time I got too drunk to make it home and she had to walk me. The many times she helped me study for tests I was sure to fail without her help. The time we dumped our terrible exes' things in a lake near campus.

Despite our distance now, she was once the most important person in my life, and if I can be there for her now, I want to be.

"You're so sweet, but I don't want to put you out. I'm sure Lowell needs you much more than I do. Parents trump divorces."

"No. No. Don't be silly. Let me talk to him. Surely we can work something out. Neither of us should have to stay here for much longer anyway." My body revolts against the lie, my core tightening as I recall our conversation about staying here permanently. "Just let me see what he thinks and I'll let you know, okay?"

"Thank you. You know I wouldn't ask if it wasn't important." Her voice breaks, and I sense the truth in her words.

She needs me.

"You'll be okay for a few days, right?" I ask gently.

"Yes," she promises. "Of course."

"Okay. Talk soon."

"Bye, friend."

I end the call, dropping the phone to my lap with a sigh.

"Everything okay?" My eyes shoot to the door, taking

in the sight of Lowell. I hadn't realized he was there. Hadn't realized he'd been listening.

"Yeah." I stand as he moves forward. "I'm sorry I ran out so quickly."

"It's okay." His hands lift, easing me into his arms. "You seemed worried. Who were you talking to?"

I pause, trying to determine how much he heard. Telling Emily I was going to ask to leave early and actually doing it are two entirely different things. Now faced with the choice to disappoint Lowell, I'm not sure I can do it.

"It was Emily again." I slip my phone into my pocket, avoiding meeting his eyes.

"Ahh. That's right. She called you the other night. Is everything okay?" He tilts his head toward his shoulder, empathy etching across his face. With his entire world crashing around him, he shouldn't be worried about anyone else, but I appreciate that he is.

"She's..." There's no point trying to hide it, even if it feels like gossiping to share the information. He'll have to know eventually if she's going to be staying in our home. "She and Grayson are separating. Getting a divorce, I guess."

"Oh, wow. That's... God, that's terrible." His words are soft. He glances toward the floor. "She must be having a tough time."

"She's okay, I think. She will be, anyway. But, yeah, it's a shock. She asked to come visit us at home, but obviously she realizes that isn't an option right now."

"Why not?"

"Well, I told her I wasn't sure when we'd be back there."

"Oh." He nods slowly, glancing around the room as if searching for something. "You meant Nashville." Worry has drawn lines around his eyes, pinching the skin into tight wrinkles. "Do you want to go back?"

"No." My answer comes too quickly. I'm not sure if he's asking about right now or ever. "Of course not. She understands I can't leave you right now. There's too much going on. I don't want you to deal with it all alone."

The stress on his face disappears. "Well, why don't you just have her come here?"

"What? *Here?*" I expect I'm staring at him as if he's sprouted a second head. "To The Pond?"

"Yes," he says, seeming more certain of the suggestion by the second. "Why not? They live nearby, don't they? Didn't they move back home near her dad after her mom passed?"

"Yeah, but..."

"I think it's a great idea. It would be less of a trip for her, but still a chance to get away, we have plenty of room here, and besides, it would give you a distraction so you aren't bored by what I'll be dealing with over the next few days." He steps closer, his hands running down my arms. "And it'll mean I get to keep you here with me."

"No. It's too much. You're dealing with a lot right now, Lowell. I appreciate the gesture, and Emily would too, but I can't ask you to do—"

"You aren't asking. I'm offering. It would be good for both of you. And it will stop me from feeling so guilty about disappearing all hours of the day and night to handle Dad and Mom's affairs."

I contemplate the possibility, rubbing my lips together. "I don't know. Would Dallas and Fallon feel like we're imposing? I don't want to overstep."

"I've told you...this place is ours now, whether we stay or leave. There's no such thing as overstepping. Besides, this place has, like, twenty-six bedrooms. There's a good chance they won't even notice she's here." He releases a long, drawn-out breath, waiting for me to agree. "Go on, invite her. It'll make you feel better." Leaning forward, he rubs his nose across mine, reading me all too well.

I sigh. "Are you sure? Because I can tell her it's not a good time. She'll one-hundred-percent understand. We have so much—"

His lips brush against mine, shutting me up. "Of all the things I love about you, your selfless little heart is at the top of my list. If your friend needs you, you should help her. I'll be fine. Everything will be fine. I'm positive."

He's right, of course. I know it the second I feel my stress melt away. My tense muscles loosen as he steps back.

"Now, I'm going back to dinner. Call her and tell her I can have Henry pick her up at the airport if she gives us her flight information."

"Thank you."

He squeezes my hand gently before dropping it. "No need to thank me. It's your house now, too."

Something about the words washes away the warmth I felt just moments ago. I scan the room—white plaster walls, marble floors. The peculiar art. The furniture that doesn't match my taste. These things can be updated, I realize. But will that change the way I feel inside this home?

Like an outsider.

Like I don't belong.

Houses have feelings. When you walk inside them, you know whether it's a happy home or...something else.

The Pond feels anything but happy. It feels nothing like a home.

CHAPTER EIGHT

Two days later, I'm waiting on the terrace when the familiar black town car pulls down the drive. Henry steps from the driver's side and zips around to Emily's door, opening it for her.

I see her black leather heel first, then her hand as she grips the top of the door to stand. She looks just as I remember her, as if time hasn't touched her in the slightest. Her blonde hair—golden and warm like a summer day—blows around her head, her flawless but minimal makeup practically magazine ready.

She smiles at me, raising her sunglasses up from her eyes and sliding them on top of her head. Her hand lifts slowly, waving.

Moving to the back of the car, Henry retrieves her bag and carries it up the walk, leading her to me. She stops a few feet away, her shoulders sagging with so much unsaid.

Apologies for how long it's been. For both of our

current unfortunate circumstances. Relief at finally seeing each other now.

I take a step forward, my arms outstretched, and gather her into a hug. I breathe in her scent—chamomile and lavender—and squeeze her tighter.

All my stress melts away against her. Until that moment, I hadn't realized how much I had missed her. How much I need her.

"It's so good to see you," she says, her voice low in my ear. When she pulls away, she grips both of my hands, dangling them between us. "You look great."

"So do you." I squeeze her hands gently and release them, then sling an arm around her shoulder, or try to, at least—I've nearly forgotten how much taller than me she is. I settle my arm around her waist, leading her into the house. Henry has already disappeared with her bag, taking it to the room where she'll be staying. "I'm so glad you could come."

"I can't thank you enough for inviting me."

I shake my head. "No need for thanks. We're happy you're here." I pause. "I was so sorry to hear about your dad."

She squeezes me tighter. "Thank you."

"He was such a sweet guy. I kept watching for an announcement about the funeral, but..."

"I know." She turns to face me. "It's okay. He wanted to be cremated, like Mom, so we didn't have a service." She blinks back tears. "Just a small memorial with family. It was so sudden, and he hadn't planned anything, y'know?"

"I wish I could've been there for you." The guilt of knowing I wasn't eats at me. She was the person I leaned on most when my dad died.

She lifts her gaze to survey the room when we enter the foyer, as if realizing how grand the place is for the first time. "Wow, this place is...really something."

I smile with a sense of pride that shouldn't belong to me. I deserve no credit when it comes to this place.

"It is, isn't it? It's a bit overwhelming, honestly. I've gotten lost an embarrassing amount of times since we arrived."

She's still taking in the room when she answers. "Good to know I won't be the only one." Her eyes finally land on me. "So, why do they call this place The Pond?"

I snort. "Apparently because it's full of Bass."

It takes a few seconds for the joke to hit her, but when it does, she chuckles. "That's hilarious, actually."

I hum. "I thought so, too."

She clears her throat, taking a step toward the stairs. "I should probably go to my room and freshen up. I'm feeling pretty gross after my flight. Is it this way?"

"Yeah." I lift a hand to point toward the second floor and the staircase to our left. "The bedrooms are upstairs." Hurrying to catch up with her, I lead the way to the bedroom the staff has prepared for her. The second door on our left is propped open, her pink hard-shell suitcase resting at the foot of the bed. "This is you." I push the door open a bit more and point to a door on the far side of the room. "All the bedrooms have their own en suites. We made sure it's stocked with fresh towels and some sample toiletries, but if there's anything you need, just let me know and I can send out for it." The language I'm learning to use since arriving at The Pond, the words coming out of my mouth—like offering to *send out* for things—sound strange and pretentious. But it's the reality, so I spit them out.

"This is perfect." Emily crosses the room and sinks down onto the bed, smoothing her hands over the duvet. For the first time, I see tears lining her hazel eyes.

"Good, I'm glad you like it." I pause. "And I'm glad you're here, Em. Truly."

"I'm glad I'm here, too." She swipes her fingers under both eyes simultaneously.

"I'll let you get cleaned up now, but I'll just be right across the hall in our bedroom if you need me. Take a shower or a nap or...whatever you need." I check my watch. "Dinner is always at six, so I'll come and get you then if I haven't seen you before."

"Okay, great." She yawns and stands from the bed, unzipping her suitcase. "Two hours to make myself presentable." She winks. "I think I can manage."

I give her a look and turn to walk from the room, already missing her the second I shut the door.

AT FIFTEEN MINUTES UNTIL SIX, I close out of the expense report I've been working on and leave the bedroom. Emily is waiting in the hallway; she has curled her hair into beachy waves and freshly applied her makeup. She smiles at me and smooths a hand over the purple blouse and jeans she's wearing.

"Oh, good." Her eyes flick over me. "I wasn't sure what to wear. I feel like I should put on a ball gown and never take it off here."

With a grin, I glance down at my jeans and ballet flats. "No, nothing like that. It just *feels* like we're in a museum."

She laughs, then loops an arm through mine. "Well, lead the way. I'm eager to see more of this place."

We're the first to arrive in the kitchen, and Emily takes in the sight of it—the unimaginably expensive dinnerware, the simple yet elegant table runner, and the candles and foliage in the center of the large, solid oak dining table. She runs a finger along its edge.

"This is amazing, Austyn. Really."

I shrug. "It is, I agree, but it's nothing to do with me."

"Not before, maybe." She gives a cocky grin. "But it's all yours now."

The voice that answers isn't mine. "At least that's what we hear."

We spin around to see Dallas standing in the doorway, observing us. The sleeves of his white button-down are rolled to his elbows and paired with black slacks; he's more dressed up than I've seen him on any occasion other than the funeral. His eyes narrow at Emily.

"Dallas, hi." I step forward, my cheeks heating. I didn't mean for him to overhear what Emily said about The Pond being mine. It feels wrong now. "This is my friend, Emily. She's going to be staying with us for—"

Dallas moves past me, cutting off my words and ignoring Emily's outstretched hand.

"Hopefully not too long. Seems there's no room for guests here, as of late," he mumbles, taking a seat in his usual chair directly across from mine.

"Did you have a nice day?" I ask, my voice coming out shaky and garbled.

"Just peachy." He scoots his chair into the table, the wood scraping against the floor, avoiding meeting either of our eyes.

Emily's eyes widen for half a second as we connect over the strange interaction, but I quickly change the subject by showing her to her seat. "You can sit next to me." I point to the chair I'm referring to.

"Emily..." Lowell's voice is warmer than his brother's, and when I turn to see him, it's a welcome surprise. It's the first time I've seen him all day. He's been locked in his father's old study, going over a ton of the company's files, and I realize then how much I've missed him.

He's the only thing keeping me feeling safe here. The only piece of home I have.

"Hey, stranger." She grins up at him and he moves past me, holding both arms out to pull her into a hug. Like his brother, Lowell is dressed in a suit. Unlike his brother, this is usual for him. He's the type of man who feels like he's dressing down when he wears a blazer and jeans.

Their hug lingers, his hand strokes her back, and when they break away, her eyes study his. "I'm so sorry for your loss."

"Thank you." He dips his head, clearing his throat, then steps back, slipping an arm around my shoulders. "We're glad you could make it."

"Thank you for having me." She tucks a piece of hair behind her ear. "I'm just sorry I couldn't make it to the funeral."

"Don't worry about it." He pushes away her concern. "It was just a small thing. Come on, let's sit." He takes his place at the head of the table, with me on the corner next to him. Pulling his chair back, he waits for us to be seated.

The door from the kitchen opens and a swarm of servers appears, making quick work to set our dinners in front of us and fill our glasses with white wine. I watch carefully, making sure they give Emily water. Before her arrival, I made sure to tell them she's sober. To my relief, they remember.

"This looks delicious," Emily says to no one in particular as she unfolds her napkin and drapes it over her lap.

I slip mine from where I previously laid it on the table and do the same.

"Thank you, Miss. It's spinach-stuffed salmon," one waiter says. "With lemon butter broccolini and creamy mushroom risotto."

Though I still have mixed feelings about having a staff, I'm learning that one of my favorite things about being here isn't the obvious thing—being waited on or having our food cooked for us—but the simple fact that I no longer have to make decisions about so many things. For all three meals each day, someone else purchases the ingredients, prepares the food, and places it in front of me.

I'm realizing how much mental energy goes into the most mundane things.

Here, it's all done for me, so I can accomplish my task list for the day, usually with time to spare.

It still feels strange to have someone picking up after me, laundering my clothing, running my errands, and preparing my meals. But, as much as I hate to admit it, I'm beginning to get used to it.

What does that say about me? That I'm sufficiently normal? Or that I'm not as genuine as I like to believe?

I'm struggling with it a lot. I never thought I'd be the kind of person who'd be so okay with this type of thing.

On one hand, apparently it's providing quite a few jobs and the workers don't seem to hate it. On the other, it's degrading. Why should they have to clean up after us? Why can't I make my own bed or cook my own food?

"Thank you," Lowell calls out as the staff disappears back into the kitchen.

I hear Fallon's voice before she enters the kitchen, the rest of her family in tow. She's on the phone with someone, discussing an issue with a fabric source.

"Yes, but I was told the shipment would arrive last Thursday and it's still somewhere outside the country. What am I supposed to do in the meantime?" She barely acknowledges any of us as she pulls out Harriet's seat. "I don't care how you handle it, just make sure you do." With a huff, she ends the call.

When she looks up, her lips flatten as her gaze lands on Emily. "Um, hi. Who are you?"

I speak up, placing my fork next to my plate. "Fallon, this is my friend, Emily. Em, this is Lowell's sister, Fallon." I meet Fallon's eyes again. "Lowell and I went to college with her. We were all friends."

"And why is she in my house?"

"*Your* house?" Dallas scoffs. "You gotta stop popping the oxys, sis. Your house is an hour away."

She forces a mockingly amused face and flips him off when the girls have their heads turned.

"We invited her," I say, keeping my voice steady. Worry seeps into my veins. "She's going to be staying with us for a few days."

In truth, we haven't discussed how long she will be staying. As long as we do, perhaps.

Unless we're never leaving.

"Hmm." She sinks into her seat, taking a sip of her wine. "Nice to meet you."

"You too." Emily is quiet, cutting into her meat slowly, methodically. She places a bite in her mouth and rests her fork on her plate while the rest of the family digs into their food.

"How's school, Harry?" Dallas asks his oldest niece.

She grins. "I got an *A* on my science test."

"Of course you did. I told you you would."

"And Mia brought me a new friendship bracelet since my old one broke." She extends her wrist, showing off the diamond bracelet.

"I like it." He winks at her. "Very pretty."

"Let me see, Harriet," Lowell says, leaning over the table to get a better look.

She holds out her wrist, twirling it slowly so the light reflects off the jewels.

"Very nice."

"Her little friend, Mia, bought all the girls bracelets for their birthdays this year, but Harriet's broke during her tennis lesson," Brent says.

"Uncle Dallas was going to get me a new one, but we couldn't find the right one." Harriet lifts her glass of juice to her mouth, taking a drink.

"Mia's mom's the designer," Fallon adds. "The line won't launch until the spring."

"Oh, watch out!" Dallas cries as Harriet moves to place her glass down, knocking it over. Fruit juice splashes across the table, the deep-red liquid staining the white table runner.

Harriet's eyes fill with fat tears.

"I'll get someone," Brent says, standing and dashing from the room while Fallon and Dallas work to contain the mess.

"It's okay, Hare," Fallon tells her.

"You were just acting like Mommy when she's had a few too many drinks, weren't ya? She spills her juice then, too," Dallas says with a grin.

Fallon swats at him playfully. "Hush."

Within minutes, a housekeeper appears in the room with Brent close behind her. She clears away the table runner, cleans up what's left of the mess, and refills Harriet's glass.

Once things have calmed down, we return to our meals as if nothing happened.

"So, Em, tell us what you've been up to. How's work?" Lowell asks, leaning forward eagerly.

His warmth toward her is something I'm grateful for. I can't help feeling bitter about how Fallon and Dallas have treated her so far.

Maybe this was a bad idea after all.

She finishes chewing the rest of her food and takes a drink of water before rubbing her hands together. "Work's fine. Busy, like this time of year usually is. As the seasonal workers' contracts end, everything is kind of flipped on its head for a while. And, other than that, well... I'm hanging in."

The smile she gives him doesn't reach her eyes.

"What do you do?" Brent asks, slipping his phone back into his pocket.

"Nothing exciting." She shakes her head. "I work in human resources for a coffee company."

"How cute." Fallon's smile is pinched, annoyingly so.

I know she's uncomfortable with us having a guest so soon after our arrival, especially given the circumstances, and I get it. Really, I do. I'm not expecting her to play hostess. But she doesn't have to be rude either.

"What about you?" Emily asks. "Do you all work in the family business like Lowell?"

"Hardly." The lines between Fallon's eyes soften. "I own the fashion line, Envo. My husband, Brent, is our COO."

"That's amazing." Emily's smile is genuine, her voice

gentle. If she's affected by their rudeness, she doesn't show it. "And what about you? I'm sorry, I don't recall your name."

"Dallas," I remind her. "Lowell's brother."

"Dallas, Lowell, and Fallon. Double *L*s in all of your names," she muses. "Clever."

Dallas doesn't look up from his plate, which is nearly half cleared. "Me? Well, I *don't* own a fashion line."

"Dallas doesn't *own* anything," Fallon points out, helping Harriet, who has spilled a bit of her juice again. "He's still *finding* himself." She waves her hand in the air as if we're discussing some mystical idea.

"Fuck off, Fal," Dallas grumbles.

"Hey!" Brent shouts, leaning forward as if to shield the children from the coarse language. "Come on, man. Not in front of the girls."

"Sorry, girls. I'm sure you've never heard Mommy or Daddy say that word, have you?" He takes a bite of his salmon and Harriet giggles.

"I was just making a point, Dallas. You *are* trying to find yourself, aren't you?"

"I don't need to own a company to know who I am." His upper lip curls with disgust. "Or an inheritance."

"There's nothing wrong with having goals, Dallas. Or having ambition. Can you ever just act as if you don't hate us? That everything about this family doesn't disgust you?" Fallon asks. "For a single day? Even if it's just pretend?"

"Sorry, Sis. Playing pretend was never my thing. You know that."

"Oh, believe me, I know—"

"Enough, guys. Come on." Lowell groans. "Can we just have an enjoyable meal together, please? Fallon and Brent brought the girls to visit and Austyn has a guest. Let's just have a nice dinner, okay?" It doesn't go unnoticed that he's only looking at Dallas.

"Sorry. Forgot this wasn't my house anymore." Dallas stands, shoving his chair back. "Great chatting with you all. I'll just go to find my cupboard under the stairs." His words drip with sarcasm as he bends forward into a bow before stalking out of the room.

"Was that a *Harry Potter* reference?" Fallon asks, stifling a laugh that no one else joins in on. "How's that for entertainment, hmm? Didn't know you'd get dinner and a show, did you?" She pops a bite of salmon in her mouth, looking slightly embarrassed. "Harriet, honey..." Lifting a finger to the edge of her lips, she motions for her daughter to wipe sauce from her cheek.

Except for the occasional babble coming from Harmony, we finish the rest of the meal in total silence.

AS THE EVENING WINDS DOWN, Lowell, Emily, and I make our way to the living room, where Lowell prepares our drinks, showing off a bit while mixing them.

He presents the pale-green cocktails with a flourish of his wrist, handing a glass to Emily.

"Virgin, of course," he says. "Austyn told me you aren't drinking."

"Thank you for remembering." She grins and takes a small sip. "Oh, this is delicious, Lowell."

He passes the next one to me.

"What's this called?" I inhale the citrus scent, eyeing the dark-cherry garnish.

"It's a *last word*."

He carries his drink to the chair across from us and we sit in front of another enormous fireplace while Emily finishes telling us about her latest trip to Spain.

"Anyway, I feel like I'm rambling. It was beautiful, end of story." She laughs, then takes another drink. "Gosh, I've missed your cocktails, Lowell."

"I've gotten better at them, thank goodness."

"You were always very good," I assure him.

"We were college kids, anyway. All we cared about was whether or not it would get us sufficiently drunk."

"I could always manage that much, at least. Man, how did the time get away from us?" Lowell says, his tone wistful and yet, somehow, filled with regret. "It's been too long."

"It has," Emily agrees, rubbing a finger along the edge of her glass. "But time tends to do that, doesn't it? Slip away. I feel like it was just last week that we were all in school."

"Last week and a decade ago all at once," I murmur.

"Well, it *was* nearly a decade ago," Lowell teases.

"Ew, don't say that!" Emily shrieks and tosses a throw pillow at him.

He catches it and tucks it underneath his arm. "We didn't know how good we had it back then, did we?"

"We knew," I say. "We just didn't realize how quickly it would all be over."

When I look up, Lowell is staring off with a strange expression on his face. He's thinking about his parents, I realize. Back then, he still had them. Back then, I still had my dad. Emily still had both of her parents. What I wouldn't give to go back to that time for just one more day.

One more day without the weight of the grief I'd have to carry for the rest of my life. The weight we all carry now.

My eyes fall to Emily. Of the three of us, she's dealing with the most pain. At least Lowell and I still have each other. I wish there was something I could do to help her.

"I used to be so obsessed with you," she says, staring at Lowell, her cheeks flushed pink.

He cuts a glance her way. "Oh, you were not."

My face burns suddenly. This is all news to me. From what I remember, Emily always had eyes for Grayson. When did she have a crush on Lowell? Why didn't she say anything?

"I swear I was." She nods slowly, then gives him a small, lopsided grin. "In college, I think I might've been verging on stalker territory before I finally worked up the nerve to talk to you. I tried a few times, but I was invisible to you back then. I was always so shy."

He laughs. "And I was an ass."

"Well, I won't argue with that." She lifts her glass toward him in agreement. "Thank goodness my best friend could see past it and fall madly in love with you anyway."

"You never said anything." I tilt my head to the side, watching her. "Why didn't you tell me?"

She tucks her legs up in the seat underneath her, slipping a hand between her knees. "Oh, because before I could work up the nerve to talk to him, you guys were assigned as lab partners on that... What was it...biology?"

"Chemistry," Lowell and I answer at the same time. When he meets my eyes, his are so full of warmth and desire I force myself to look away, heat creeping up my neck.

"Right, you were partners on that chemistry project, and I could tell you were already crazy about each other, anyway." She shrugs. "There was no point. Besides, Grayson and I always made more sense."

"You guys were great together," Lowell agrees. Do I hear a hint of jealousy in his voice?

No. I have to be imagining it.

Her smile is sad. "Were." She repeats the word. After a beat, she yawns and stands from her chair. When she stretches, her shirt rises to reveal a bit of her flat stomach.

I can't resist the urge to watch Lowell, to see if he's noticing her. To my relief, I find him staring down into his glass, swirling the pistachio-colored liquid methodically.

"I should head to bed," Emily says. "I'm still catching up from the early flight. Thank you, guys, again. Dinner was great. This place is...really amazing."

"Do you want me to walk you up?" I ask though I find myself not wanting to.

"I think I can remember the way." She places her empty glass down on the side table and brushes my hand as she moves toward the door. "Good night."

"Good night," Lowell and I say at the same time. When I look at him again, his eyes linger on the empty doorway, as if searching for the woman who just passed through it.

CHAPTER NINE

I adjust under the comforter, pulling it up to my chest and resting both arms on top of it just as Lowell appears from the bathroom. Like always, he's undressed down to his boxer briefs, his hair freshly brushed. He lifts the covers, the cool air from the room hitting my skin, and slips into bed.

"Mmm." He hums, rolling to face me with his eyes closed and a smile on his lips. "How was your day?"

"Fine." I sigh. I shouldn't be angry right now. Really, I shouldn't. I don't even know why I am. "How was yours? Did you hear anything back from the police?"

"Yeah. It's handled." His eyes open.

"Handled how? As in closed or...?"

"Yes, the case is closed." His hand slides across the covers to rest on my hip. "I told you I'd take care of it."

"But if it is...what does that mean?"

"It means their wills can finally be carried out." His eyes search mine for an answer I'm not ready to give. Not ready to discuss. "Mr. Bingham will be by the day after tomorrow. And once we've gone over all the details, he'll register the papers with the courthouse or...whatever he does, and once it's all done, the deed for the house will transfer to us. Er, well, me for now, but us after the wedding. The paperwork has already been established to make me CEO officially. Didn't need the will for that part."

He can't contain his grin, and it makes the last of my bitterness fade away. "It's all coming together." His hand pulses on my hip, tugging me to him gently.

"It's all you've ever wanted." My voice is low. "I'm so proud of you, Lowell. Your parents would be, too." Though I don't know them, it feels like the right thing to say. We're in a weird place right now, a sort of limbo where we have to grieve everything we're also celebrating.

He swallows. "They asked me today about moving our stuff to the primary bedroom."

"Who did?"

"The housekeepers. Now that it's officially going to be ours, they suggested we get set up in their room, but I'm not sure I can do that, you know? It's the biggest room in the house, so I want it, but...it was theirs. I can't *not* see them in there, you know?"

"I get it." I brush my hand over his temple, moving the hair back from his face. "There's nothing wrong with this room. It has plenty of space for us. Leave their room alone for as long as you need."

"I think I will. This actually used to be the primary

bedroom. Did I tell you that? Before my parents combined two bedrooms to convert their room into an updated owner's suite."

He's rambling now, trying to break into the conversation we haven't finished about the house.

"No, you hadn't told me."

He laughs nervously, his eyes searching mine. "Have you...thought any more about staying here?" He lifts my hand to his lips, placing delicate kisses against each of my fingers.

"Not really. Today's been so busy with Emily's arrival. And I had to call Ramona to go over the end-of-the-month reports, plus place an inventory order."

Something flickers in his expression, but it's gone just as quickly as it appeared. "It's good for you that Emily's here, I think. Another familiar face. I know this can't have all been easy for you."

"I like having her here," I say, though the words weigh on my tongue with the bitterness of a lie. *Is it a lie?*

I used to be so obsessed with you.

Her words—something about them, something about the way she was looking at him when she said them—make me feel sick.

"I like feeling as if I'm helping her."

When I don't feel like I can help you. I don't say the last part out loud, but somehow, I think he can still hear it. Feel it. He's always been able to read me.

"Me too." He squeezes my hip again, inhaling deeply.

"It was...kind of weird that she mentioned having a crush on you before, don't you think?"

"Was it?" His brows dart together. "It's not like she has a crush *now* or anything. It was years ago."

"Yeah. I guess so."

"I think she was probably just reminiscing and feeling sad about Grayson. I'm sure she didn't mean anything by it."

"You're probably right," I whisper.

"Hey, you aren't bothered by it, are you? Who cares if she had a crush on me—I mean, can you blame her?" He chuckles, pulling me closer. Brushing his nose across mine, the laughter fades from his eyes. "I chose you, Austyn. That's all that matters."

I close my eyes, willing myself to believe him and let this go. Maybe I've just had too much to drink. I'm being paranoid. His lips touch mine, gently at first, but then the kisses come faster.

More aggressive.

His hand slips up my shirt, and when he presses his body to mine, I feel the evidence of his desire against my thigh. His mouth leaves mine, kisses traveling across my collarbone and to my chest before moving farther south. He lifts the covers to disappear underneath them completely, and it's only seconds before I feel his hot breath against the bare skin of my stomach.

He tugs my pants off, the warmth of his mouth quickly replacing them right where I need him.

My heart thuds in my chest, heat spreading across my body.

He groans against me, my body going slack as the sensation takes over.

He chose me.

Not her.

I'm in his bed right now.

She's alone.

I shouldn't be thinking about this at all, I know, but I can't help it. Even several minutes later, when he's on top of me, our bodies slick with sweat and bucking together with an urgency we haven't had in months, I can't help thinking it's the first time we've had sex since we arrived.

Can that really be a coincidence?

CHAPTER TEN

The next morning, when I wake, the house is still quiet. The scent of breakfast hasn't yet permeated the upper floors of the house, and other than Lowell—who's up at the crack of dawn every day, without fail—I'm fairly certain it'll be a few hours before everyone else wakes.

Usually, I'm a six o'clock person. Lowell's up and out the door by four, but he's pretty good about not waking me. I sleep until six and then I'm up and at the bakery before I open it at seven thirty.

Today though, I'm not sure what woke me. Checking the clock, I see it's just after four. Perhaps Lowell was less than quiet after all. Or perhaps I found no peace in my dreams.

For a while, after my dad died, I had trouble sleeping. I hoped to see him in my dreams, prayed and begged for it even, to the point that I couldn't fall asleep. I thought something was wrong with me, because when I slept, I didn't see him.

Until one day, I did. It was the first full night's sleep I'd had in a long time, and I dreamed of him. When I woke up, it was like losing him all over again.

Finally, I understood and appreciated the time it took before I saw him in my dreams. If it had happened in the early days, I'm not sure I would've survived it.

In the years since, I've readjusted to a routine and my sleep patterns are predictable. Which is why waking up so early bothers me.

I glance up at the ceiling.

It's this place.

I know it.

Something about this house is disrupting my sleep. It's messing with my moods.

I hate it here.

The words echo in my mind.

I *hate* it here.

I shouldn't. Lowell loves it. This is his home. It could be my new home. This shouldn't be such a big decision. If it's about Mom, I could easily move her in, too. She'd come with me, I'm sure. And seeing how Lowell has been with Emily, I know he wouldn't care.

So, what is the issue?

Out of bed, I brush my teeth and wash my face, taking my birth control as I try to force the thoughts away. I need to finish my monthly reports and check in with the store again to make sure everything's running smoothly in my absence.

In the closet, I search through my clothes. As I pull a shirt from the hanger, another falls to the floor and I reach for it.

"Shoot." I tug the shirt, thinking it will be easy enough to retrieve, but am met with resistance. I bend, trying to get a closer look at what it's stuck on and spy a small air vent in the wall.

On my hands and knees, I crawl for the back of the closet, using my phone as a flashlight to see what the button has snagged on and how to free it.

Near the vent, I can hear the cleaners vacuuming in another room. Finally, I have an eye on the problem and place my phone down. The string is caught on a corner, where the two planes of metal meet.

I ease it forward slowly, but there's not enough room for my fingers to pull it free. This sweater is one of my favorites; I have no desire to ruin it if there's another way.

I push up from the ground and return to the bedroom, searching through my makeup bag for—*there it is*. The small metal nail file should work to unscrew the top of the vent, just enough for me to wiggle the button free.

And that's exactly what I do, using the flat end of the file to turn the screw over and over until it's loose enough to slip the button out, sweater unharmed.

I breathe a sigh of relief and begin turning the screw back into place. When I'm done, I move to stand but realize my phone flashlight is still on. From this angle, as the light passes over the vent, something catches my eye.

A glint of something.

I ease down, flat on the ground, and shine my light through the slats.

What the...

A book of some sort, with metal edges, lay just feet from my face, fluttering from the circulating air as it moves around it. My heart pounds in my ears, my throat dry as I sit back up, using my file to remove the screw again, then the other three.

I'm singularly focused on this task, my thoughts racing. When the vent is loose, I place it on the ground quietly and reach inside. Dust collects on my arm as I reach through the cool metal shaft for the book.

When my fingers connect with the leather of its cover, I drag it free.

It's lighter than I expected, smaller somehow too. The cover is a deep-green leather, and both right-hand corners are decorated with metal embellishments.

I run my fingers along the edges. There is no title. No author name.

This is not a book.

I open to the first page, confirming my suspicions. Across the delicate, yellowing front page in a scratchy, handwritten font, I scan the words with a ball of fear swelling in my chest.

> This diary belongs to Celine Mason, age 16.
> DO NOT READ!

CHAPTER ELEVEN

CELINE'S JOURNAL

This diary was a sixteenth birthday present from my parents. Apparently, I'm coming to an age where I might start having a lot of feelings.

I thought it was a dumb present, honestly. I'm not one of those whiny girls who needs to detail every thought they ever have.

Then, yesterday, a week after my birthday, they dropped the bombshell.

I guess when your family tells you they're uprooting your entire life, forcing you to leave the house you've always lived in, and dragging you to live with a group of total strangers, you're allowed to have a few feelings.

I'm not sure how much I'll use this thing, really. Especially since I'm going to start working now. But...it feels pretty cool to tell you how much I hate this.

If I hadn't made it clear:

I HATE THIS.

I miss my friends.

And my grandparents.

And my home.

And my bedroom.

The place we're going to be living now is strange. The people who live there are strange.

They're rich and powerful, Mom says, and they need us. They could change everything for us. Make sure we never go without again. Without food. Water. Make sure my clothes always fit.

I don't care about any of that, but the money Mom and Dad will be making here will help us be able to take better care of Grandma and Grandpa, so I guess I shouldn't complain. They took care of us for my whole life, and now, with Grandpa sick, we have to return the favor.

I'm only dealing with it because I love them.

My parents will flip their lids if I mess this up for them.

So, I won't.

Even if I hate it at this new stupid place.

Even if I hate the new stupid people.

And their stupid house with its stupid name.

What kind of dork wants to live in a place called The Pond anyway?

CHAPTER TWELVE

AUSTYN

I don't know why I do it.

I have no idea why, but when I hear someone approaching the bedroom door, my first instinct is to rush to shove the journal under the dresser and push the vent cover back into place, turning one screw with my finger to keep it from falling out.

I stand up just as I hear the bedroom door opening.

"Babe? You up— Oh." It's Lowell. "Well, she must've already woken up."

Who's he talking to?

"Where'd she go?" Emily's honey-smooth voice carries through the room, a hint of amusement in her tone.

"No idea. Come on in." He lowers his voice. "Austyn? Babe?" He says the words, but just barely. Like he's not actually looking for me at all. Like he hopes not to find me. I should shout out and tell him I'm here, then walk out of the closet and reveal myself, but something keeps me firmly planted in place. "Maybe she's in the bathroom."

"I don't need her that badly," Em says. "I can catch her later."

"Is it something I can help you with?"

She chuckles. "I'll just wait for her. Thanks, though."

"What? You don't think I can help?" he teases.

Each laugh from her is as if I'm dousing myself with ice water. "I wouldn't exactly expect you to be up to date on women's fashion, no. Besides, I know how busy you are."

"Not too busy." Their voices are getting farther away. "Come on. I'll take a look."

I see my chance then, unwilling to sit still any longer. I grab my headphones from on top of the dresser and stalk from the closet, just in time to see them exiting through the doorway.

"Oh, hey." I lower my headphones, putting on my best shocked expression.

"There you are." Lowell rests a hand on the doorway as they both turn back to face me. "We were looking for you."

"I didn't hear you. I was listening to a podcast. Is... everything okay?" My eyes fall to meet Emily's.

"I was trying to decide what shoes to wear with this outfit, but I didn't want to wake you. Lowell said you were probably awake."

"Oh." I swallow down the bitterness I feel. This is ridiculous. I'm being ridiculous. "Sure, I'll come help you decide."

"Thanks."

Lowell takes a step back, waving at us over his head and disappearing down the hall. I turn back to Emily, following her lead to her bedroom. "So, are you planning on going somewhere today?"

"I thought I'd run into town for a bit. I need to pick up some things I couldn't bring on the plane. You're welcome to come with me if you'd like. Girls' day." She shimmies her shoulders.

"I should probably get some work done this morning. What time were you planning to leave?"

"I'm in no rush. I can just hang around here for a while."

"It's up to you."

She approaches her closet and pulls out two pairs of shoes but hesitates. "Is...everything okay?"

"Why wouldn't it be?" I ask, looking for a hint of guilt in her eyes.

"No reason, I guess. You just seem kind of...out of it."

"I'm fine." I force a yawn. "Just tired." How can I tell her how badly her comments bothered me last night? She'll think I'm being absurd. I *am* being absurd. Or worse, she'll feel bad about it and decide to leave. I don't want that either.

What *do* I want, though?

For everything that happened last night to never have happened. For the seed of doubt not to have been planted in my head.

After a moment, she sighs, slipping each foot into a different shoe. "Okay, which one?"

IT'S JUST after noon when I've finished the reports and head down to the dining room to find Emily, Lowell, and Dallas gathered around the table. The staff has placed a spread of lunch meat, cheeses, and various breads on trays across the table.

"Hey there, stranger." Em grins up at me. "All done with work?"

"I'm at a stopping point for the day, anyway." I sit down in a chair, trying to avoid the nagging worry in my gut. Why were they all in here without me? What were they talking about? Why is it that Lowell hasn't had time to stop for lunch with me since we arrived, and yet here he sits, laughing it up with Emily like he doesn't have a care in the world?

"Want some?" He tries to pass me the tray of bread, forcing me to focus on the task at hand. I take it and begin preparing my lunch.

"Anyway," he goes on, finishing a story I didn't hear the beginning of, "it turned out the bouncer was the woman's husband. He caught them right in the middle of it, outside behind the bar. Threw him and his band out. Needless to say they never came up for the second half of the show." He shakes his head, smearing mayonnaise on the slice of bread in his hand. I've heard this story before, so it shouldn't bother me. Dallas looks just as annoyed as I do, which makes me feel a little less alone. "Craziest thing I've ever seen."

She's hysterical, laughing until her face is red and eyes are watering. "Wow. You swear that's true?"

"I swear."

"Man, you think you know a guy."

"Yeah, well, it was before he was as big as he is now, but still. I can't look at him the same way. Can't listen to his music without picturing that husband just—wham!" He mock-punches his own jaw.

"It's all so very LA." She dons a fake accent. "Celebrities behaving badly."

"Hey, guys?" I say too loudly, slamming my hand on the table to interrupt their laughter. Dallas nearly spits out his mouthful of food. With the room silent and all eyes on me, I realize I actually have no idea what I want to say. Nothing at all. My mind goes totally blank.

I just needed them to stop laughing.

"Uh, yeah?" Lowell asks.

I say the first thing that comes to my mind. The wrong thing. The very wrong thing. "Do you know who Celine Mason is?"

Three blank sets of eyes blink back at me.

"Who?" Lowell asks first.

"Celine Mason," I repeat. I can't tell him how I know the name. I don't want him to know about the journal until I've read it, and to be honest, I'd basically forgotten about it until this exact moment. He's waiting for me to explain, but I have nothing to say.

"Nope. Never heard of her," Lowell says. Is he lying? I'm not sure I'd know. "Why do you ask?"

"Oh, I—"

"Hey, Lowell, don't you have to get that paper sent back to Mr. Bingham?" Dallas stands, checking his watch.

"Uh, yeah, but not until the end of the day. Why?"

"Well, I'm leaving now, so if you need my signature today, we should go do that before I'm gone."

"What's the rush?" he asks, checking his own watch. "You didn't mention going anywhere today."

"This is me mentioning it." Dallas wipes his lips with his napkin before balling it up and tossing it onto his plate. "Hurry up. Can't evict me if you don't get the paperwork done first." The joke is dry and humorless, but Lowell stands anyway, carrying his sandwich with him.

"I had Henry warm the car, so it's ready whenever you are. You girls have fun." He kisses my cheek as he slips past.

"Thank you."

"This is delicious," Emily says, staring up at me over the trays of food. "I can't believe they feed you like this for every meal."

"They're just sandwiches, Em." I don't mean to be so rude, honestly, but I'm bitter and frustrated, and I can't seem to shake it.

"Fair enough. I'm really excited about our girls' day." She changes the subject like a champ. "I need to get a few things—namely, my acne medication. I had my doctor call in my prescription to a local pharmacy. If I don't use it, my face will be covered in breakouts by the end of the week. I'm sure you remember how it used to be."

I give a halfhearted smile. In college, Emily battled acne, but it was no worse than the rest of us.

"Thank goodness we left so much back in college, hmm?" I take a bite of my sandwich, letting the words and their meaning hang in the air between us as I hear footsteps heading back in our direction.

"Austyn?" I look up, expecting to find Lowell, but I see Dallas instead. I never realized how similar they sound. "Lowell asked me to come get you for a sec."

I bristle at the idea of being summoned like a dog. Why can't he come to me? Without a word, I place my food down and dust off my hands. Then I stand, making no effort to hurry, and cross the room.

In the foyer, before I can reach the stairs, Dallas grabs my arm.

"*Ow!* What the hell are you—"

"Why are you asking about Celine Mason?"

"What?" Panic sets in. Why is *he* asking about Celine Mason? Who is she? Why did I have to mention her?

"Where did you hear that name?"

"I..." I can't tell him the truth, either. No one can know until I understand what's going on. It's the only power I have in this entire situation. "I don't know."

"Dallas? Everything okay?" Lowell's voice echoes through the hall from the floor above us, and Dallas pushes me backward into the wall underneath the stairs.

His eyes meet mine, mouth hanging open.

Dallas puts his hand on the wall beside my head, his face inches from mine. "Where did you hear that name, Austyn?"

"I...don't remember." I can't remember anything at the moment. His smell is intoxicating, and in this dark, secret space, I'm getting lost in it.

He's too close.

His eyes too dark.

Too locked onto mine.

When he opens his mouth to speak again, I can't help staring at the little dent in his bottom lip.

What is wrong with me?

"Dallas?"

Without an answer, Lowell is moving closer to us. He's on the stairs above our heads. Dallas leans closer, his head next to mine so he can whisper in my ear.

"He's going to ask you how you know about her. Tell him you saw her name on a gravestone outside."

"What? What are you talking about?" I whisper.

"Dallas? Did I hear someone scream?" He's getting closer.

"Tell him you saw her name on a gravestone. However you know her name...tell him that's how. And don't tell him about this." He pushes back away from me, releasing my arm, and I suck in a full breath for the first time in what feels like a lifetime. "Don't tell him I told you anything."

"But you *haven't* told me anything—"

Dallas presses a finger to his lips, silencing me, and jogs back up the stairs before Lowell appears. "Sorry," he shouts. "I had to get a drink."

It's a dumb excuse. He's not returning with a drink,

but I guess Lowell doesn't notice because moments later, I hear the door to the office upstairs shut.

"Everything okay?" Emily's standing in the doorway to the foyer. How long has she been there? What did she overhear?

I put a hand to my stomach. "Yeah, sorry. I... I'm sorry. I'm not going to be able to go with you, after all. I forgot I had some other things to get done for the bakery."

"Oh...okay. Are you sure? Anything I can help with? Maybe we could knock it out together and still have time to go?"

"No," I say so fast I practically cut her off. "But thanks. Maybe next time. Henry's waiting out front, so you can leave whenever you're ready."

"Okay..." Her voice is soft. She seems disappointed. "I'll see you later, though."

It's not a question, but I nod anyway. "Yep, later. I'm, um, I should go." With that, I turn and jog up to my bedroom. I shut and lock the door behind me with one question screaming in my mind: *Who the hell is Celine Mason?*

CHAPTER THIRTEEN

Celine Mason was seventeen years old when she died.

That's just about all my internet search reveals.

Seventeen. A year older than the age she was when she got the journal. When she moved to The Pond. For all I know, the journal may be the only known account of what happened to her that year. How she died.

Was she sick?

Did someone hurt her?

The only other thing I'm able to uncover is a link to her tombstone, which Dallas was right about, it is somewhere in the Bass family's private cemetery.

I close the laptop and make my way into the closet, easing myself onto the floor. I realize I half expect the journal to be missing, for it to have never existed at all, as my hand connects with the leather.

But it does. It's there.

Pulling it out, I lean back against the wall behind me and flip it open.

Okay, Celine. Tell me all your secrets.

CHAPTER FOURTEEN

CELINE'S JOURNAL

Okay, so maybe I don't hate it here.

My first month at The Pond hasn't been as bad as I expected. Things are so different here and I'm very busy, but I don't hate it.

Mr. Bass gave me a job to do. I help clean his office every day before school, and then I have to help clear away and wash the dishes after dinner. It's not bad, and I'll get paid actual money starting tomorrow—my first official payday!

Mom and Dad say I have to put it back and save for when I'll need a house of my own, but I don't think it will hurt to spend a little bit. Maybe I'll get my ears pierced like Sarah, but they'd be furious if they found out.

Anyway, aside from Mom and Dad, there are some cool people here. There are a few kids, but most of them are younger than me. Rosie lives across the hall, and well, she's younger but still kind of fun.

And Mr. Bass is really nice to me, too! I thought he wouldn't be because he has so much money and this huge house, but he's actually funny and kind of normal. Mrs. Bass is another story. I don't think she likes me all that much, but I haven't given her a reason not to. I clean up after her and the baby whenever I'm told, and I always make sure not to make a mess.

It's so lame.

I'm counting down until I can walk out of here for good. Just two more years.

I'll write again soon, diary!

CHAPTER FIFTEEN

CELINE'S JOURNAL

Guess who finally has, for the first time in her life, her very own bedroom! If you guessed me, you'd be right!

Living at Grandma and Grandpa's, I always shared a room with Mom and Dad, so I didn't mind it when we had to do that here (at least I had my own bed and not just a mattress on the floor), but yesterday, when I was cleaning Mr. Bass's office, he told me he thought I'd earned my own. This afternoon when I got home from school, it was waiting on me!

I feel strange, in a way. I'm the only kid here who has their own room. Lots of the other housekeepers have kids, and Dione, the cook, has two little boys. The drivers all live in separate cabins on the grounds, like the groundskeeper

Mr. Tuttle, so their kids probably have their own rooms in those cabins. I'm not sure. But either way, inside the residence, I'm the only kid with her own room.

I'm also the oldest kid, so maybe that's why.

Practically an adult.

But still. Today, Rosie didn't want to play after school. Mom says not to let it hurt my feelings, so I won't. She's only twelve anyway, so who cares what she thinks?

I'm just better than her. Rosie doesn't have her own job like I do. That's her fault. When she's older, she'll understand.

Speaking of, Mr. Bass asked me to start coming back to his office after dinner. He says there's more that he needs me to do for him.

File things, I guess. He says I'll make a great secretary someday.

I don't mind it so much, honestly. I like working with my hands.

When I tell him that, he always laughs.

I like his laugh.

It reminds me of Mr. Puglisi's, from school. They're both handsome too, but Mr. Bass is kinder.

I should go.

God, I'll die if anyone ever sees this.

CHAPTER SIXTEEN

AUSTYN

I run my fingers across the folded envelope resting inside the journal, easing it out and unfolding it carefully. In neat penmanship, the envelope is addressed to Celine Mason from Dorothy Mason.

The letter inside is simple and sweet, telling Celine how much she misses her and how proud she is of her for getting a job. She jokes about her grandfather and asks about her parents, then tells her to call soon.

The sound of someone moving outside my bedroom door causes me to jolt. I push the letter back inside the envelope and place them both into the journal before shoving it back underneath the dresser. Then, I stand, jogging into the bedroom just in time to see Lowell entering the room.

"What were you doing?" he asks, brows drawn down.

"I've been working." It's not an answer. Not really. But he doesn't press me on it. Instead, he shuts the bedroom door behind him. I move back to the chair, lift my laptop from it, and sit down, watching him closely. "Everything okay?"

"Yeah, everything's fine. I was just coming to check on you. I thought you were going with Emily."

"Oh, no. I realized I still needed to put in the supply order for the store. We were low on a few things when I got the inventory report last night, and it totally slipped my mind."

"Can't Ramona handle that?"

"She can, but I always do it. Besides, she's handling everything else while I'm away. It's the least I can do." I tap my fingers on the metal top of the MacBook.

His lips purse with unsaid words, but he sinks onto the edge of the bed, studying me.

"What?"

"Don't you think it's time to go a little more *hands-off*?"

The question comes out of the blue. "Uh, no. Why would I do that? Delia's is my bakery. My dream. I have no desire to let it go."

"I didn't say let it go, I just..." He puffs out a breath of air. "Never mind. I just thought you'd like to relax and spend time with your friend instead of worrying about work."

"We'll have plenty of time to spend together."

His hands go up in surrender. "Okay, sure. Forget I said anything." Still, he doesn't leave.

I open my laptop, trying to get him to take the hint and go away. I need to keep reading that journal.

"Hey,"—he snaps his fingers as if something has just

occurred to him—"I meant to ask, why did you ask me about Celine Mason earlier? Where did you hear that name?"

I freeze, glancing up at him. "What?"

"At lunch, you asked about someone named Celine Mason. Who is she?"

I flash back to what Dallas said. His warning.

I have no idea whom to trust, but I go with my gut. "Oh. Um, I don't know. I remembered seeing her name on a headstone in the graveyard. She was young when she died... It's just been bothering me. I wondered what happened."

"Oh." Is it me, or do his shoulders visibly go slack? "Oh, okay. I guess I never noticed. The name doesn't seem familiar. Honestly, I don't know most of the people out there. It goes back generations."

"She died in the seventies, so it would've been recently."

He shakes his head. "Hmm, you'll have to show me sometime. The name's not ringing any bells."

"Okay. I just thought I'd ask."

He turns like he's going to leave, then spins back. "Could you put a pin in that for a few hours? I could really use your help with a few things."

My hope deflates, my chance to read anything else from Celine disappearing. "Sure."

For now, apparently, the journal and all its secrets will have to wait.

CHAPTER SEVENTEEN

In the office, Lowell has me helping him check over a few of the papers from the attorney and posing as his secretary to make a few client phone calls when that's done.

It's not the first time I've done clerical work for him or the last, I suspect, but it's the first time it has annoyed me. It's as if he knows what I'm trying to do and wants to keep a close eye on me.

But why?

The thought crosses my mind that this could all be a setup somehow. What if Lowell set me up to see if I'd find the journal? What if he's watching me to see what I'll do? If I'll be honest with him about what I've found. It seems far-fetched. How would he have ensured I found the journal, anyway? It was an accident. Still, I guess it's possible this is a test after all. If so, I'm failing miserably. Then again, why would it be okay for him to do that?

If someone watched our relationship from a distance

over the years—an unbiased third party silently observing our every waking moment—I have to wonder whose side they'd be on up until this point. There's no doubt they would've switched teams a few times over the years. When I lied to him during our senior year so I could go on that camping trip with my friends rather than attending the show his band was putting on, they might've been angry with me. Maybe they would've even called me selfish. I couldn't blame them. Perhaps, when he argued with me about going to see my parents instead of using the tickets to the hockey game he'd surprised me with for the week before my father died, the person would have sided with me then. Maybe they would've told me I deserved better. That I should leave. Throughout the years, throughout our various difficulties, the highs and lows, I have no doubts that anyone would've had trouble sticking firmly on my side—or his, for that matter. But I wonder now...whose side are they on?

Could I be accused of being selfish to an outsider's eyes? Childish, maybe? Am I being rude to Emily? Or cold to Lowell, who just lost both of his parents rather suddenly?

I can't help feeling judged—by my inner voice, if nothing else. But I do not know how to shake this feeling.

I've never felt so alone.

There I go again, right?

Don't worry, I wouldn't blame anyone if they're firmly on Team Lowell. Maybe I would be, too, in their position. Maybe he's the only rational one in our relationship.

It certainly feels like that lately.

Either way, as we work, I'm quiet, my mind racing with everything that's happened lately.

Lowell's back is to me, his gaze firmly locked on the window as I end my latest call.

"They're back," he says, taking the stack of papers from my hand. "That's probably enough for today. Do you want to go see if Emily needs any help?"

"Won't Henry do that?"

He snorts. "Okay, you little workaholic. Only room for one of those in this family." He shoos me with the papers before placing them down. "I'm giving you an out. Enough work for the day. Go have fun with your guest." His chin juts toward the door.

"Are you sure? I don't mind helping you finish up. Then we could go to dinner together."

"I'm positive." He's already sitting down in his chair, phone to his ear. "I didn't mean to keep you this long anyway. I just have a few more things to handle, and I need to get the papers emailed back over to Mr. Bingham. Speaking of, if you see Fallon or Dallas, would you have them come see me?"

"Sure." I take a step back, then another as he turns away from me. Within seconds, I'm back out of the room and in the hallway.

"Hey!" Emily, despite being out of breath from trekking up the stairs, sounds as energized as ever when she sees me. "Just the person I was looking for." She extends her arm, wiggling the many bags in her hand. "I gotcha something."

"What?" I search behind her for a sign of Henry, but he's not there. "Where's Henry?"

"Oh." She waves a hand. "I told him not to worry about it. I just had a few things. Come on, come on. I want to show you this." She grabs my arm, tugging me down the hall and into her room, where she plops four bags down on the bed and retrieves the small, pink gift bag from the bottom of the pile. "Here, open it."

I take the bag apprehensively. "You didn't have to get me anything."

"I know, but I saw it and thought of you. Besides, just think of it as a thank-you gift for putting up with me for a few days." She sits on the bed, pulling one leg up to remove her shoe, then the other. Her blonde hair falls loosely from her ponytail as she does.

Reaching into the bag, my hand connects with something soft. I pull the olive-green chenille sweater out, running my fingers over the cloud-soft fabric. "It's..." I lift it up to my cheek. "Wow. This is really nice, Em. You didn't need to—"

"I know." She shakes her head. "I wanted to. I saw it and just had to get it for you. It's not much, but it's the least I could do."

"Well, thank you." I place the bag down and fold the sweater carefully, slipping it back inside. "Really. I love it. You know me so well."

"Always have." Her smile is softer now. The sweater reminds me of a younger version of myself. Of a time when the sweater would've been too expensive for my college budget, and Em would've bought it just to surprise me. Not that she was wealthy growing up—far from it. She and I were both middle-class kids with enough money to get by but never enough to thrive. We went to college on full-ride scholarships. But, in college, Em's job had paid better than mine. And I'd been helping with Dad's medical bills when I could. Her mom was sick then, too, but her parents had better insurance.

So, she'd often surprise me with gifts that were far too nice and too expensive for a college kid to truly appreciate them.

Suddenly, my eyes are watering for a time that has long since passed. Why am I letting my jealousy get the better of me? Here I am, in a house with my best friend for the first time in the five years since graduation, and I'm letting her silly little comment ruin all our fun?

If I had anything to worry about, she wouldn't have mentioned it. That's so clear to me now. I know Lowell and Emily. I trust them. They'd never do anything to hurt me.

"You okay?" she says, reading my expression.

I nod, dropping next to her on the bed. "I'm just having a rough time with things."

"I thought so. You've been distant today... Anything you want to talk about?"

"I don't even know where to begin." It's the truth, but I begin anyway, "First of all, Lowell wants us to stay here."

"What, here? *Here*, here? Permanently?" When I

nod, she goes on, "How would that even work? With your mom and your job?" The skin around her eyes wrinkles slightly as she studies me. "Is that what you want?"

"I have no idea what I want, honestly. Of course, I want him to be happy. I don't want him to feel like I'm making him give up something that's so important to him."

"The family home?"

"Among other things, yeah. The house, the job, his family. If we stay here, he can become CEO of the company. I'm not sure how well he'll be able to run things from Nashville. But this is supposed to be his." I glance around the room. "How can I tell him no?"

She rests her hand on my leg. "You *also* have a house, a job, and a family back in Nashville. Isn't that the same thing?"

"It doesn't feel the same, no. Mom could move here, and the house isn't our forever home. We always knew that." I sigh. "I could always open a new bakery near here. And you're here, so that would be nice, too."

She presses her lips together. "As much as I would love to have you close by, what I want more is for you to be happy. Did he ever mention that he might want to move back home after his parents died?"

"I don't think he thought it was anything he'd have to worry about for a long time. We never really discussed it. Maybe after the wedding we would've, I'm not sure... But now it's happened and we have to decide, like, right now."

"Have you told him you're unsure about it?"

I drop my head forward. "How can I do that? He's so excited about this, Em. I just need to wrap my head around it, I think."

"Easier said than done." Her thumb rubs circles across my knee. "Maybe you should just talk to him. Tell him your reservations. You could open a new bakery, sure, but you're already established there. This is a totally different market—"

"Maybe I could just run the one in Nashville from here, then. Hire extra help. It's not like I need to be hands on, really. And we don't need the money, so I don't *need* to open one here."

"But you'd want to."

"I can't tell if that's a question."

"Is that an answer?"

"Opening a new one or running the old one from here, either way, I'd be doing it out of sheer stubbornness. Anything I make financially would be a drop in the bucket compared to Lowell's income. I know it seems silly, but...I just don't want to give it up. I worked so hard to make Delia's what it is. I'm not ready to walk away."

Her head tilts to the side, and she squeezes my knee. "Talk to him, okay? He loves you. He'd want to know if you're having second thoughts about all of this. With Grayson and me, we swept so much under the rug and left too many things unsaid. That just leads to resentment. Trust me, you want to have this conversation now. Not ten years from now. Even if the end result is the same, at least he'll understand your feelings better and be able to help you through them."

I place my hand on top of hers with a sad smile. "I'd forgotten all about our therapy sessions."

She tosses her head back with a laugh. "I was going to be a therapist, remember?"

"I certainly gave you enough practice."

"Yeah, well...things don't always work out like you plan."

"It's not too late."

She's quiet for a minute, then breaks eye contact with me, easing her hand back. "Maybe not. But that's a decision for another day. I should get all this unpacked before dinner."

"Right." I stand and turn for the door, but before I reach it, I hear her voice again.

"Hey, are you sure there's nothing else bothering you?"

I pause. "No, that was it."

Her nod is slow. "Okay. I'll see you in a bit, then."

I'm not sure why I lied, why I'm protecting the secret about Celine. All I know is I think I've stumbled onto something big, and until I understand what it is, I can't tell anyone.

CHAPTER EIGHTEEN

After dinner, I return to the office where Lowell has been working all day. He headed straight for a shower after our meal, so I have a bit of time, though I'm not sure how much I'll need.

I tap the mouse on his desk twice, waking up the screen of the desktop computer sitting there. I wonder how often his father sat here. Having only seen pictures of the man, I can't picture him. I can't picture him working in this office or living in this house or giving his son a pat on the back, for that matter. I'll never know the man my husband came from, and that bothers me.

At least Lowell got to meet both of my parents.

In college, the Bass family never came to visit, and Lowell rarely went home. They thought he was being ridiculous by obtaining a degree he'd never need to use when he had a perfectly good job at Bass Industries waiting for him. I think there was a bit of a falling-out for a while and

Lowell needed space or to prove something to himself, but by the time things had cooled down, he and I were falling in love and he was building a life in Nashville with me.

I'd talked to them on the phone, of course, even FaceTimed once...sort of. *Well, Lowell FaceTimed them and I walked through the background and waved.* His family wasn't close like mine, and I accept that. Still, I always thought there would come a day when I'd be sitting around the dining room table with them or spending Christmas Eve around the enormous Christmas tree Lowell always talks about.

Now, all chances of that happening are gone.

Shoot.

When the screen comes on, I realize I don't know the password to this computer, as it's still set up under John Bass's account. I have no way of seeing the email from the lawyer or understanding fully what accepting this house will mean.

Tonight, I'm going to talk to Lowell about my hesitations over moving into the house, but in order to do that, I need to fully understand what we're being given, and I can't seem to get straight answers from Lowell lately. I want to read the emails for myself.

Sighing, I lock the screen and stand up. Lowell's laptop is still in our room. I should've tried to read them from there first, but it would mean more risk of being caught. At least from here, I have a semblance of warning when someone is coming down the hall.

In our bedroom, he could catch me at any moment.

And I can't take his laptop away; it would look even worse if he caught me somewhere hiding with it.

Deciding quickly, I dart across the room, out the door, across the hall, and back to our bedroom. The shower is still going when I dip my hand into the space between the bed and the nightstand where his laptop bag rests and pull it open.

I place the silver MacBook on the bed and flip the screen up, type in his password, and click on the browser to open his email. Scrolling through his inbox, I search for his lawyer's name.

Bingham.

Bingham.

Bingham.

The first email that catches my eye mentions a Clark Bingham, but is sent from Wes Barnum, his accountant. I open it.

Monthly expense report attached.

The email is short and concise. Dry.

It's not what I'm looking for, but I can't help being intrigued.

I click on the attachment and spy a payment to Clark Bingham and Associates.

Lowell and I have separate accounts, of course. We'll combine them after we're married, I'm sure, but for now, it just makes sense to keep them separate. So, while I know he is rich, the number at the top of the screen feels like a ball of dough has lodged in my throat.

$8,654,718.06

I freeze, scrolling down through his various expenses. There are those for the house, our mortgage payments and utilities, all except the electric bill, which I've always insisted on paying.

Jesus, I should've let him take care of it after all.

He paid his lawyer twenty-six hundred dollars at the end of the month like his accountant said, but it's another transaction that catches my eye.

Or, better yet, another name.

Emily Campbell

I stare at the number.

The amount.

Why had he paid Emily thirty-five thousand dollars?

It feels as if an icy palm has gripped my lungs, its hold unrelenting. I close out of the email and change my search. Now, I'm looking for anything that includes Emily's name.

I hit "search" and wait.

Within seconds, my screen is full of emails containing expense reports.

Last month...yep. Thirty-five thousand to Emily Campbell.

The month before. Thirty-five thousand to Emily Campbell.

The month before that. Thirty-five thousand to Emily Campbell.

What the hell?

What the hell?

He's been paying Emily the same amount every month for as far back as the inbox goes. Over three years.

Thirty-five thousand dollars, apparently, is nothing to my millionaire fiancé, but it's *not* nothing to Emily. It's a huge amount of money. Is that how she's been able to afford to travel like she does?

Does Grayson know about this?

What on earth could the money be for?

The bathroom door opens—I hadn't registered the sound of the shower shutting off moments earlier—and Lowell appears in the doorway, torso glistening, towel around his waist.

"What are you doing?" He uses another towel to dry his neck and face, scrutinizing me. He's caught me red-handed, but I can't bring myself to care.

"Why are you paying Emily thirty-five thousand dollars every month?" The words come out in a blur, and I watch his face shift from confusion to anger, then back.

"What are you talking about? Is that what she told you?"

"No." I spin the laptop around. "I'm seeing it for myself, Lowell. What is it about?"

"Look, I have no idea." He bends down, staring at the screen. "It could be a different Emily Campbell. It's not like it's an uncommon name. I'll have to check with Wes. It's probably something for work."

"Why would a work expense be coming from your personal account?"

He groans, slamming the laptop shut. "I don't know, Austyn. I said I'll check. Why are you going through my accounts, anyway? I thought we said we weren't going to be those people? Thought you said you didn't care about my money?"

I reel back as if I've been slapped. "I don't care about your money, Lowell. If I haven't proven that by now, I'm not sure I know how to. But I do care about the fact that my fiancé is sending colossal sums of money to my best friend without my knowledge. How can you explain that?"

He shakes his head. "I've already given you an answer. I have no idea what it's about, but I will talk to Wes and find out. Either way, in case you've forgotten, my parents just died, so maybe don't do this right now, okay? I've got a few other things on my mind." He begins to walk from the room, but he stops himself. "You know, if you don't want to stay here with me, you could just say that. You don't have to start a fight for the sake of it. If you want to go back to Nashville, just go!" His hand swings toward the closed bedroom door, an invitation to walk out.

"Is that what you want?"

"Of course not!" he bellows, his neck flushing pink. The veins of it are all bulging with anger now. "If that's what I wanted, I would've never invited you to stay. Would've never proposed. I want *you,* Austyn. I've never stopped wanting you. But ever since we arrived, you've done nothing but push me away."

"You sprung it all on me, Lowell."

"Sprung what?"

"*Everything!*" Now I'm up off the bed, shouting back at him. "The house, the new job, the long hours, and now...and now this." I point to the laptop. "I don't know how I'm supposed to take this." My voice cracks, and I hate it. I drop my head, my eyes pooling with tears. When I look back up, there's no power to my words. "Just please... Tell me the truth. Are you having an affair?"

The blood drains from his face, his mouth going slack. "Am I *what?* Are you... Are you serious right now?"

"What else am I supposed to think?" I lift my hands to both sides in an exasperated shrug.

"You're supposed to think that I'm your fiancé and that I've never given you a reason not to trust me. That we've been together for nearly a decade and I've proposed to you. That I love you." His shoulders slump. "I guess none of that means as much to you as it does me."

"Wait, Lowell—" When he walks past me, I reach for his arm, but he jerks it from my grasp.

"Let me go. I just need a minute." He spins around once he reaches the door. "You need to think long and hard about whether you want this, Austyn—me, this house, this family, any of it. If you don't, just..." His head tilts to the side, the blues of his eyes like light reflecting off an ocean. "Just be a grown-up and admit it, okay?"

HE DOESN'T COME BACK to our room until well past midnight. By this point, I'm still tossing and turning in bed, trying to make sense of what I've discovered.

There is no world in which I see it as a possibility that

the Emily Campbell in his ledger is not the same Emily Campbell sleeping across the hall.

I should march into her room and ask her, but I'm empty. If I ask and she has some excuse, or worse, denies it outright, then where will I go? I'll just look like the crazy one while they move on with their lives.

I pretend to be asleep as he slips into bed. I'm sure that's why he's waited so long to come back, anyway. Hoping to avoid another argument. He rolls over, his back to me, and within minutes, I hear his soft breaths turn to light snores.

He always could fall straight asleep. Meanwhile, I lie awake for at least an hour remembering and obsessing over every terrible or embarrassing or slightly awkward thing I've ever done.

Remember that time you, for a brief second, missed an armhole in the sleeve of your cape at the salon? Pretty sure your hairstylist hates you now.

I consider waking him, trying to have the conversation again now that we've both calmed down, but it seems like an awful plan. What would I even say to him that would be different than what I've already said?

Nothing.

There's nothing to say.

I can't possibly lie here any longer, I decide and slip out of bed. A walk would be nice. Anything other than this room where I feel as if I'm suffocating and drowning all at once.

That's when I remember the journal.

I walk into the closet and, without flipping on the

light, crouch down on the floor. I reach my hand under the dresser, searching for the leather, and when I finally land on it, I slip it inside the waistband of my pajama pants and head for the door.

The house is quiet, which is an odd state to find it in. Usually, it's buzzing with the sounds of its dozens of inhabitants. The dishwasher humming, the vacuum in a distant room rumbling, hushed voices, footsteps here and there, doors shutting.

But now... Nothing.

My footsteps are louder than I expect on the marble floor.

Thwack.

Thwack.

Thwack.

The marble is cold on my bare feet, but I can't turn back now. I hurry down the stairs and then the hallway, careful to move as quietly as possible to make my way into the study.

The fire is still going, as it always is, which seems unsafe now that I think about it. I sit down in the oversized blue armchair, tucking my feet up under me and moving to raise my shirt.

"Finally ready to stop denying how badly you want me, hmm?"

His voice causes me to jump, and I jerk my shirt back down in an instant.

I check over my shoulder to my left, where Dallas is sitting up from a reclining position on the small sofa near the far wall. Slapping a hand to my chest, I huff out a breath. "You scared me." My heart thuds in my ears, cheeks burning with embarrassment. "What are you doing in here?"

He closes the book he'd been reading. "Oh, sorry, am I not allowed in here anymore? Your future husband didn't mention what rooms were off-limits yet."

The hurt is evident in his words. "Dallas, I'm sorry about all of this. I didn't know Lowell was going to ask you to leave. I'm sure he'll come around if you just talk to him."

He smirks, then lies back down, opening the book again. In the dim light, I can't make out the title. "You obviously don't know my brother that well, do you, Tex?"

"Tex?" I frown at him. "Who's Tex?"

"You are." He peers around the book at me, looking pleased with himself.

"I'm lost."

"Oh, come on. Texas is clearly the first thing everyone thinks of when they hear Austyn."

"That's not true." My tone is adamant.

"Oh, really? It's not? What do you think of, then?"

I'm quiet for a minute, thinking. "Jane Austen, maybe? Or Austin Nichols. He plays Julian on the show *One Tree Hill*."

He eyes me. "You want me to call you *Jane Austen* or *Austin Nichols*?" One brow rises. "Do you even know how nicknames work, Tex?"

"I *want* you to call me Austyn, which is my name. Besides, you do understand the irony of *you* saying this to *me*, right? If I'm Tex, then you're Tex, too."

"Aww. Is this our *Notebook* moment?" He stares up at the ceiling with a wry grin, clutching the book to his chest.

I roll my eyes, looking away. "You're insufferable."

"And you're miserable."

I cut my gaze back to him. "Excuse me?"

"You don't want to be here. Admit it." He pushes up on his elbows, closing the book again. "You hate it here."

"You know nothing about me." I swallow down the truth like a shot of whiskey. It burns like whiskey, anyway. "And I don't hate it here."

"Could've fooled me."

"Well, you don't exactly seem to sing the place's praises either," I point out.

"Oh, no. Did you miss my little Bass family song and dance number at eleven?" Dark hairs stick out at the wrists of his waffle-knit sweater as he checks his watch. "Pity. It was sold out."

"I'm serious. Why do you even care about staying here if you hate it so much?"

"Who says I care about staying here?"

"You certainly seem like you're in no hurry to leave."

"Yeah, well, looks can be deceiving."

I glance away, mumbling, "I couldn't agree more."

"You know,"—he sits up, his words straining with the effort—"you should be careful who you trust around here, miserable or not."

"What's that supposed to mean?" I bristle at his comment.

"Exactly what I said. Not everyone is your friend here. Including those who pretend to be."

"Like you?"

He smirks again, pushing off the sofa and standing with a yawn. He moves across the room slowly, my throat dry as I wait to see his next move. When he lowers himself in front of me, all dark eyes, taut arms beneath a fitted shirt, and intense, minty cologne, he's quiet for a moment. His hand comes to rest on the back of the chair above my head, the other just beside my thigh. He leans in so slowly I stop breathing, stop thinking or comprehending what's happening.

I've never been so present in a moment in all my life.

When his face is inches from mine, his eyes flick to my lips. His nose brushes mine. I'm frozen in place, but my body is on fire.

When he speaks, his voice is so low I almost miss it. "I never said I wanted to be your friend."

"Well, good thing you're not."

He bites his bottom lip, seeming to know what he's doing to me and enjoying every moment of it. "Keep telling yourself that, Tex."

He pulls back at once—moment over—and disappears from the room without looking back.

I sit there for a moment, catching my breath.

The room is silent except for the crackling of the fire. My gaze flicks to the sofa where he was only moments ago. It's as if I dreamed it all up.

In fact, maybe I did.

I check over my shoulder, then stand and cross the

room, fully aware of how wrong and ridiculous this is. I sit down gently, checking the doorway again, then lie down. My body is in the exact position his was. The sofa is still warm from his body heat.

The shiver that sends through me isn't normal.

I close my eyes, turning my head toward the cloth cushion and inhale deeply. His cologne is ingrained in the fabric and, with my eyes closed, it's easy to pretend he's still here.

My breathing grows shallower as I think back to the way he stared at me, the indention in his bottom lip, the way he bit it.

Another deep breath.

This is so wrong.

My hand slides up my thigh, imagining it's his hand. Heart racing in my chest, face on fire, my fingers slip under the edge of my shirt.

I inhale his scent again, falling deeper into the fantasy. My fingers climb higher up.

Shit.

My hand connects with the cool leather of the journal, still resting against my stomach. The blood drains from my face as I sit up, mortified by what nearly just happened.

What the hell is wrong with me?

CHAPTER NINETEEN

CELINE'S JOURNAL

Mr. Bass invited me to dinner in his office tonight. He says he wants to go over a few things and thinks it would be better if we could sit down and talk.

Mom and Dad aren't sure it's a good idea. They want to be there. But I promised them I'd be on my best behavior. Besides, this is my job and I want to make sure I've earned it.

They're the ones who insisted we come here in the first place, didn't they?

Now that I've got my own room, I feel like I never see them. I wake up early to clean the office, then hurry to school. When I get back home, I do my homework, have dinner with the rest of the kids here (sometimes my parents, if they aren't still working, but they usually are) and then I'm back to cleaning the office again before bed.

The Basses let me take every other weekend off so I can see friends from school or relax, but it's not like I have a ton of friends, just Judy, but her mom doesn't like her to spend much time with me. She hasn't said that, but I can tell.

After Christmas, I went to see a film called The Exorcist. Mom and Dad would be furious if they knew, but it was far out! I'm going to invite Billy Allen to see it with me again soon. He's cute and makes me laugh. Sometimes…I think about kissing him.

I CAN'T BELIEVE I JUST ADMITTED THAT.

It's so embarrassing.

But we'll keep this between you and me, right, diary?

Anyway, I should go. Lots of homework before dinner with Mr. Bass! I'll write again with an update soon.

CHAPTER TWENTY

AUSTYN

"Oh, I'm sorry, ma'am."

The voice startles me, and I slam the journal shut. One of the housekeepers is staring at me strangely from the doorway, dressed in her nightgown and robe. She's familiar to me, someone I've seen around the house, but I'm unsure of her name. Her curly, dark hair is usually pulled back in a tight bun, but now it's loose around her face.

"That's okay." I adjust on the sofa, wondering how much she's seen. "Is there...something I can do for you?"

"I didn't mean to interrupt. I can come back." She hesitates. "It's just... Mr. Bass always had me put the fire out at two." She points to the clock on the wall, telling me it's nearing two a.m. "But if you're using it..."

"No." I get up quickly, dusting off my clothes. "No. I should go to bed, anyway."

"Alright. Good night, ma'am." She steps to the side to let me pass her, but I stop.

"Actually, I have a question for you." I pause. "What is your name?"

"Jo, ma'am. Josephine, but Jo." Her smile is kind.

"Jo, I'm trying to find out more about someone who used to work here."

Her nod is hesitant. "I've worked here all my life. Since I was a little girl."

"Did you ever hear anyone talk about a girl named Celine Mason?"

She stares at me, her face still. "No, I don't think so," she says finally.

"Are you sure? She was seventeen. Something may have happened to her. I'm just trying to find out—"

"I don't know," she says again, her voice soft, but she's walking away from me. "I'm sorry. I really should get this fire put out. Good night, ma'am."

Her back is to me as she works to put out the fire, spreading the smoldering ash with the small cast-iron shovel near the hearth. I follow her, lowering my voice.

"No one would have to know you told me. If...if you know something. I just want to help." I swallow, watching her face. She's refusing to look at me, her gaze trained on the dying fire as the light fades from the room. "I think something bad may have happened to her, Jo. Would you know anything about that?"

Once the fire is out, we're bathed in darkness. Only the glow of the moon through the pale curtains illuminates the space. It takes a moment for my eyes to adjust, but when they do, I realize she's staring at me from where she stands.

Either of us could turn on a lamp, but I don't dare move.

"I'm sorry, ma'am. I don't know that name. I should get back to bed. Early morning." She turns from me then, her robe dragging on the floor as she moves across the room and leaves me standing in the dark.

CHAPTER TWENTY-ONE

When I wake the next morning, there's a note on the pillow next to me in Lowell's handwriting.

> *Family meeting. 8 a.m.*
> *Downstairs study.*
> *It's important that you're there.*

I check the time and find that it's just after six. Even after my late night, my body refuses to sleep in.

I take my shower, contemplating what the so-called family meeting could be about. Part of me hopes he'll address my suspicions about the affair. Prove to me that he and Emily have nothing going on. Fight for me. The other half will be mortified if that's what his plan is.

After I'm out of the shower, I dry off, dress, and blow-dry my hair before heading downstairs. When I arrive at the study, Emily isn't there. I'm not sure whether to feel angry or relieved over that fact as Lowell stares at me from behind the desk.

It's odd seeing him here when I'm so used to now seeing him behind the desk in the upstairs office. That one, the one the Bass men have used as an office for many years, feels cold. Lifeless. Formal.

Here, in a room I assume is mostly decorative, I feel comfortable. It's cozy, even with the oversized desk taking up most of the right side of the room. The rest of the room is filled to the brim with bookshelves, plus the fire-place and armchairs, bookshelves, and a bar cart. It's my favorite room in the house, but now, it's tainted by what happened last night.

Just thinking about it, heat rises to my neck, and I put a hand up to cover it.

Lowell clears his throat. "Morning." He hardly looks at me as I sit down in the chair I'd been seated in last night. I flash a glance at the sofa and lock eyes with the man sitting on it.

I avert my gaze in a hurry, my throat like a desert. Dallas is sitting on the sofa, leaning forward over his legs, elbows resting on his thighs. He gives me a mischievous grin when he catches me staring, and I can't help thinking he can read the guilty look on my face.

I turn my body away from him in my chair to face the opposite side of the room. My pulse is pounding, and I feel unable to catch my breath.

Across from him, in the direction I'm now facing, Fallon sits in an armchair that nearly matches mine. She's dressed in a white-and-black pantsuit with oversized sleeves that makes her look more like she's planning to announce the chosen tributes for *The Hunger Games* than attend a family meeting.

Lowell's footsteps move toward me, though I can't see him at first from behind my chair, and then he appears. He stands in front of the fireplace with a terrifyingly serious look that says he's going to tell us we'll all be required to sacrifice our firstborn to his cause.

"Thank you all for coming." He fiddles with a button on his shirt.

"Some of us had no choice." Dallas groans.

"Fallon, can you...not?" Lowell ignores his brother and turns his attention to his sister, who is popping her gum loudly, her eyes still glued to her phone.

"Sorry, just one...more minute. There." She pops her gum again and places her phone down beside her, folding her hands and dropping them into her lap. "You have my full attention, Your Majesty."

Lowell gestures to the stack of papers in his hand. "Everything's agreed to and finalized. Everything we talked about. I wanted to have this meeting so we could... discuss everything. All of us." He looks around the room. "Should there be questions or concerns, now is the time to voice them."

He passes around the stacks of paper, one to each of us. It's mostly gibberish, a bunch of legal stuff I don't understand.

Testator...codicil...executor—that one I know—*...residuary estate...*

"Now then, since we've all come to an agreement,

Mr. Bingham says things will move much faster. It's all laid out in Mom and Dad's will how they wanted things to be handled. Privately, first of all. Between us." He waves the papers around in a circle. "So"—he's reading now—"the house will go to me, as the eldest. When Austyn and I marry, it will be ours. I will take over as head of the company and receive all of Dad's shares in Bass Industries. His stocks will be split between us three ways. The rest of the estate, and our inheritances, will be split with Dallas and Fallon taking forty percent each and me taking just twenty percent. With the house and pay raise for me, it makes us about even." His eyes skim the rest of the pages, flipping through them. "I, that's... Yeah, that's the fundamental stuff. Does anybody have any questions?"

"Mom's teakettle collection." Fallon raises a finger.

"It's yours," Lowell says. "It's in here under your section of the estate, along with all of her jewelry. The art will stay with the house like Mom and Dad wanted. The wine collection stays, but you guys are welcome to take some, of course. Dallas wants Dad's cars. The furniture will stay for now, and we can donate their clothes."

They're quiet for a moment, each of them skimming over the papers in their hands.

Finally, Lowell stares at me. He clears his throat. "Do you have any questions, Austyn?"

All three Bass siblings look at me. I shake my head, glancing back down at my papers as if I understand a word of what they say. "I don't think so."

Finally, Dallas claps his hands together. "Well, if we're done here, I guess I should start packing."

He stands, and no one stops him as he moves from the room. Within seconds, Fallon is up too, phone in hand. "Are we done? I have a call with *Vogue* in an hour."

"We're done." Lowell is still staring at me as Fallon departs the room. When she's gone, he moves to sit down on the sofa.

"Lowell, I—"

He holds up a hand, cutting me off. "Please. Let me talk."

I pinch my lips together.

"I'm sorry about the way I acted last night. You had every right to ask about those transactions and to be suspicious. I should've been more understanding. I was just stressed. I *am* stressed. But it's no excuse. You've been nothing but helpful since we arrived, and I know it's been a lot on you. I'm sorry. I know we need to have a conversation about the house and...about our future. I promised you we would and we will. I guess I'd hoped that you'd get here and fall in love with the place. That I wouldn't actually have to convince you to stay. That you'd,"—he places the papers down on the coffee table and takes my hands in his—"that you'd want to."

"It's not that I don't want to be here with you, Lowell. Of course I do. But this is all new to me. And lonely. I miss my mom. I miss my friends. I miss spending time with you...*just* you. I miss who we used to be."

"I miss that, too." He releases a deep breath through his nose. "But I'm not the same man you met in college.

Or the same man I was when we graduated. Just like you're not the same person. That's what relationships are. They're putting up with all the changes and the hard work. Bad days, good days, everything in between. Isn't that what we agreed to?"

My eyes shift to the sofa. "Yeah, it is..."

"Look, I told you when we first arrived that if this isn't what you want, I'd give it all up. I meant that. Is that what you want me to do? I can call Bingham back right now, have him change the paperwork. Or draft up papers for us to give it to Fallon. I'm not sure how it all works, but I will figure it out if that's what you want."

It's my turn to put up a hand to stop him. "We just need to have a conversation about what staying here looks like. I mean, I have a job back home. Friends. Mom."

"Your mom can move in," he says. "Say the word, and I'll have her stuff brought here by tomorrow. I'll send the company jet. She can have her own wing. East wing. West Wing. We can have some acreage cleared out and build a house for her if you want." He gives a soft, hopeful laugh. "And your friends, too. They can come whenever they want. Haven't I proven that with Emily?"

Her name sends a block of ice down my spine. He sees the shift in my emotions as soon as it happens, his shoulders straightening.

I release his hands. "You need to tell me what's going on with her, Lowell. Why are you paying Emily?"

He stands, moving back to his desk and picking up a new piece of paper. When he returns to me, he places it in my lap. "It's all a misunderstanding. See? I received this from Wes this morning."

I stare down at the image of an email resting in my lap.

Lowell—$35k to Emily Campbell on 15th of each month is monthly payment for office cleaning and cleaning and staging of new properties for Bass Industries, as per the contract I've attached, signed by you and Ms. Campbell, October of 2015. Call if you have more questions. May have been coming out of the wrong account? Send over a new ACH form if so. Thanks.

Wes

When I look back up at him, it's as if he's handed me the golden ticket. His eyes sparkle with delight. "See? I was right. It was just a mix-up with her name. *This* Emily Campbell is a cleaner here in Cali. When we hired her, there must've been a mix-up with the account numbers. I'll get it sorted with our accounting department." He tips his head toward me. "She's not the same Emily—not our friend. It's just a common name."

My chest deflates. I should feel relieved, I guess, but instead, I'm embarrassed. He'd been right all along, and I'd been angry and bitter. I'd let my jealousy and insecurities get the better of me.

"I'm so sorry, Lowell." I drop my head forward, surprised to feel tears stinging my eyes.

"Oh, honey." He pulls me into his chest. "Don't be

sorry. I understand why you were worried." He kisses the side of my head. "You know I love you. That I'll always love you. You have nothing to worry about." He gently lifts my chin, placing his hands on either side of my face so his thumbs rest on my cheeks. "I would never do anything to hurt you. You know that, don't you?"

"Of course I do." I close my eyes as cool tears spill down my face. "I feel like I'm all over the place right now." This is the man I've loved for nearly a decade. Why am I letting my fears and insecurities get the best of me now? Since his parents' deaths, and especially since our arrival at The Pond, vulnerability has weighed me down. I don't feel like I belong here. I don't always feel welcome. But those are my issues, not Lowell's. He's dealing with so much, I can't expect him to read my every thought and recognize the insecurities I'm feeling. "I'm sorry. I'm so embarrassed."

"Don't be. *I'm* embarrassed. I've been so busy since we arrived, I should've known you were feeling out of sorts. I promise to be better." He swipes a tear from my cheek. "How about we have dinner tonight? Just the two of us? Like a date."

"I'd like that."

He kisses me gently, his arms wrapping around me, and I sink into him. It's easy to love Lowell. I've always found it so effortless to trust and believe him.

How had I forgotten that?

And why am I still having so much trouble doing it?

CHAPTER TWENTY-TWO

CELINE'S JOURNAL

I can't believe it.

I really can't believe what I'm going to write.

I'm in love, diary.

So, so desperately in love. I've never felt this way before. I've never been looked at like he looks at me. I've read about it in books, seen it in films, but never once has anyone made me feel this way.

My heart just sings when I'm with him. And when we're apart, he's all I can think about.

The hardest part is...I can't tell anyone. Not even my friends at school.

They wouldn't understand. No one would understand our love.

When I last wrote in this diary, I'd never even been kissed. Now, I've done SO MUCH MORE.

It's been six months since my dinner with Simon. That night, everything changed between us. He told me I was pretty, diary. He gave me this hairbrush with little diamonds along the back. REAL DIAMONDS! It must've cost more than everything I owned combined, but it's nothing to him. I've been using it to brush my hair every night before bed. Every night before he comes to visit me.

The first dinner, he just told me I was pretty and gave me the gift, and then a small kiss before he sent me back to my room. I was over the moon that night, thinking of him, and he was thinking of me too.

He's been in love with me since I moved in, but Mrs. Bass controls him. He has to sneak around to see me. He's told me he doesn't want to be married to her anymore, and that he's told her just that, but the old witch won't hear of it.

She can't stand the fact that her husband loves me. That he's in love with me.

That I'm younger and prettier than she is. That I make him happier.

It doesn't matter, though. Soon enough, he'll leave her and we'll be together. I just have to be patient.

Diary, I'd wait all my life if that's what it took.

I love him.

I love him.

I love him.

For now, I'm hiding the hairbrush in a vent in Rosie's bedroom so Mom and Dad don't ask questions or think I stole it. And I'll keep you hidden too.

For now, this is our little secret.

CHAPTER TWENTY-THREE

AUSTYN

I slam the journal shut, staring around the empty bedroom in disbelief. Around me, the house buzzes with its usual noise. As if life is anything close to usual at the moment.

I think back over what I've read, my heart racing.

Is it possible? Truly?

I have no reason to suspect Celine of lying, and of course, men do worse things every day, but I find myself holding Simon Bass to as high a standard as I hold Lowell to.

I'd hoped he was better than this.

That the blood that runs through my fiancé's veins was better than this.

I finally had the idea to look up Simon's headstone after I returned to my room, discovering that he was born in 1954, which means he was twenty-four when Celine died. Just seven years older than her. If they'd been in their twenties or thirties, the age difference would've been minuscule. Does that make it better?

She was still a minor.

How is any of this possible?

My head hurts as I try to piece it together, but another insistent thought pops up: *What if this is all a lie?* What if it's some sort of setup or test?

I can't bear to think about it.

If it is, it means Lowell's lying to me.

At this point, I'm not sure I'd put it past him. He's made it clear he needs to know he can trust me should I become part of this family. In a weird way, I wouldn't blame him for doing it.

I want to read more, but before I do, I need to know if any of this is real. If it's true.

There has to be a way to find out more about Celine. Lowell has been wholly unhelpful and Dallas is keeping tight lipped. I could ask Fallon, but odds are she'll be just the same.

If there's anything to hide, if they know the truth about what their family did to Celine, whether they hurt her, I'm not sure they'd ever tell me.

If there's one thing I understand about the Bass family, it's that once you're a part of it, they'll do whatever it takes to protect you.

Whatever it takes, barring letting your own brother stay in your house, apparently.

I think back to the previous night, recalling my encounter with the housekeeper. The way she acted makes me think she had to have known something. She was too strange, too reserved. And the look on her face when I'd said Celine's name...it was as if she'd seen a ghost.

Suddenly, I have my plan.

Returning the journal to its hiding place, I exit the bedroom and head for the stairs. I have no idea what to expect from the third floor. All I know about it is that it's where the staff lives.

I'm relieved to see there are hardly any immediately obvious differences upon my arrival. The decor on this floor matches the previous two floors—the art, the curtains, the red-and-tan floral hallway runner. The biggest difference is that there are more than double the number of doors in this hallway.

The way it looks, the room sizes must be less than half of what ours are. I think back to the journal and Celine's mention of entire families living in the same room. Surely that's not still the case.

I take a hesitant step forward, heading toward the sound of a running vacuum cleaner. When a door swings open farther down than where I was headed, the housekeeper from last night appears. She startles, quickly moving a hand to her chest.

"Hi, ma'am." She glances around, looking for someone else. "Is there something I can do for you? Residents rarely come to this floor."

I move toward her. "You're Jo, right? I'm sorry to bother you—"

"You're no bother, ma'am," she says quickly. "What is it?"

"I just had another question for you."

The warmth from her expression dissipates.

"I'm not sure if you remember me from last night, but I had asked about—"

"I remember."

I nod. "R-right. Great. Okay. Well, I know you didn't remember Celine, but I wondered if you knew someone else? A little girl, she would've been younger than Celine. Her name was...Rosie? Maybe Rose or Rosa?"

"I don't understand," she says softly. "Why are you looking for her? What has she done?"

"Nothing." I put both hands up quickly. "Nothing at all. I've... I think she may help me find Celine's family. I think they knew each other."

"Why would you think that?"

I shake my head. "It's complicated."

"My mother did nothing wrong." Her voice is firm yet shaky. "She worked hard for this family. To give them a good life. To give me a good life."

"Your mother?" My eyes widen as I process her words. "Your mother was Rosie?"

"Yes." Tears brim her kind, brown eyes. "But she's gone. Died seven years ago. So, I'm afraid she can't help you."

"Is there anyone else who might've known her? Someone who worked here during the time your mom did? When she was still young?"

"I don't know." She shakes her head. "I'm sorry, ma'am, but I have to get back to work. You'll get me into trouble."

She moves past as I step out of her way. "I don't want to cause any trouble," I whisper to her. "I just want to know the truth."

She keeps walking, refusing to turn back. With her, the last thread of hope is torn away.

She moves down the stairs, her shoes clicking on the marble, and I'm left alone in the hallway. Just before I walk away, I glance at her door. It's a long shot, but if there's a chance this was once Rosie's room, if it's passed down through the generations, there's one last possibility for me to confirm Celine's story, even without the help of someone who was there.

I suck in a deep breath, accepting the fact that if I'm wrong, or if there's someone else in this room, I could be kicked out of the house, and possibly out of the family, for good.

At the very least, I'll have a hard time explaining what I was doing.

I reach for the brass door handle—original, probably—picturing Celine—the Celine in my head—doing the same thing.

Without allowing myself to overthink it, I twist the handle.

Click.

The door opens and I step inside, still in utter disbelief it worked. Inside the room, I finally see all the differences. The room is smaller than I expected—only large enough for what looks like a full-size bed and a small upright dresser with a flat-screen TV resting on it. A door to my right must either be a closet or bathroom, but I won't snoop any more than I have to, to find out. On the floor, there's a stack of clothes and a stuffed rabbit.

Does she have a child that lives here with her? If so, they must be kept very quiet. I never hear any children here, aside from Fallon's girls. My mind is on the journal again, picturing the meals Celine described with Rosie entirely differently now. Were they spent eating in silence or in forced whispers? My heart aches for the little girls whose childhoods should've been so much more.

I don't have time for this.

Reminding myself of the pressing issue at hand, I search the room for vents. To my relief, there are only two. One is a large return vent. Someone would open it often to replace the filter. I turn my attention to the smaller one near the head of the bed. It's rusted and gray and likely never touched. Realizing I have nothing to open it with, I rummage around on her nightstand, feeling relief when I find a penny next to her lamp.

I use it to twist off the screws carefully. My heart pounds with every twist, sure that at any moment, I'm going to see the doorknob turning and come face-to-face with the occupant of this room.

I wipe sweat from my brow with the back of my hand and continue working.

Come on.

Come on.

Come on.

I mentally will the screws to loosen faster.

When the last screw is free, I pull the rusting metal

vent down, wincing as it groans, and bend my head to peer inside.

There.

It's not possible.

I didn't know it until this moment, but I never actually expected to find anything. My breathing hitches as I reach inside, outstretching my fingers to connect with the object just inside the vent. Light from the window reflects on the diamonds as I bring it out into the room.

I turn the brush over in my hand, scanning the bristles with trembling, icy fingers. My entire body vibrates with adrenaline.

This is it. It's exactly like she described.

The pain in my chest feels like heartbreak. I'm affected by this story, maybe more than I realized.

As I hold the brush in my hand, staring at the strands of dark hair, strands that must've been Celine's, my eyes blur with tears, a lump forming in my throat. This is the brush Simon Bass gave to his sixteen-year-old housekeeper when he began having an affair with her. Raping her, if I want to get technical.

This is the brush he gave to her just months before she died.

I feel as if I'm going to be sick, but this is the proof I need.

This proves everything Celine said is true.

CHAPTER TWENTY-FOUR

I walk back to my room in a bit of a haze.

Any second now, I'm sure I'm going to pass out or throw up. I have the brush tucked safely into the pocket of my hoodie as I head for my bedroom, but a noise stops me.

I spin to my right to see Dallas standing at the foot of his bed, tossing things into a box. He stops, sighs, and runs his hand through his hair with a look of unease.

It's strange seeing him here, in his room. Strange to see his room at all, if I'm being honest. Somehow, as I study the sharp lines of his jaw, the darkness of his eyes, I can't picture him sleeping.

It seems too peaceful for someone like him.

The walls are all covered in exposed wood planks, and there's a floor lamp next to a matching set of brown leather armchairs by his window. A stack of books rests on the metal side table.

"Can I help you?"

I dart a gaze toward him, realizing he's caught me staring. "S-sorry." I tuck a piece of hair behind my ear. "I was just..." I shake my head. "Sorry, are you seriously packing? Already?"

"Were we not in the same meeting? The house is yours now, Tex. Maybe not legally yet, but it's coming. May as well get ahead of it. You can hold off on the going-away party, thank you very much."

I step forward, gripping the frame of the door. "Have you tried to talk to him? You know I'm not the one asking him to do this, right?" My voice is low. "This isn't what I want."

"What do you want?" His brow rises. "I'm not sure you've decided that yourself."

I glance down at my feet, wrapping an arm around myself. "I may not have it all figured out, but I don't want Lowell to kick you out. This is your home. Way more than it is mine. And it's plenty big enough for you to stay."

"Well, you'll have to talk to the man of the house about that." He drops a few more folded sweaters into a box and closes the flaps, securing packing tape over the top. Then, he drops the box on the floor, his voice going serious. "I'll be fine. Honestly. I'll land on my feet. I just hope you won't miss me too much."

I'm not buying into the jokes he's making to avoid feeling this. "Where will you go?"

"We own a few family homes. There's a brownstone in New York I thought I might visit for a while. I have some friends out there." He shrugs, grabbing another box from the stack next to him and unfolding it. "Look, as cute as it is, I really don't need you to feel sorry for me, okay? I just came into enough money to buy the entire rest of the neighborhood if I wanted. I could move in right next door. So, while my brother is being an ass for making me leave, it's his house and his right. That was the agreement."

His tone is sharp, but I recognize the hurt in his eyes. "You're still having to leave your home."

"It's just a building. Just sets of walls." He grabs a paperweight from his nightstand, weighing it in his hand before placing it on the bed and reaching for the stack of books instead.

"I'll talk to him, okay?"

"I don't need you to—"

"I will anyway."

His eyes flick up to mine.

"I will talk to him."

He smirks. "If I didn't know any better, I'd think you wanted me to stay or something."

I let out a laugh. "Isn't that what I just said?"

"You said you don't want me to leave. You didn't say you want me to stay."

"Is there a difference?"

"Oh. There's a huge difference, and you know it. In one scenario, you want me. In which case, Lowell will *definitely* want me to leave."

"Don't get too full of yourself. I'm just trying to do the right thing here."

"Is that it?" His focus is no longer on the box but on

me. Wholly. He takes another step forward, his cocky stare burning my skin.

"What else would it be, jerk?" I turn to walk away, but he grabs me. His body is too close. His hand grips my wrist as he leans down, his face next to mine, cheek brushing my cheek.

"If I didn't know any better, I'd say you were wondering if you chose the wrong brother." The words send lightning throughout my body. "Thinking of me when you're with him." My breathing hitches, my body suddenly rigid with heat. I should move or pull away or tell him what an idiot he is, but I can't seem to do anything. He leans closer, his breath hot on my ear. "Imagining it's my lips you're kissing. My hands on your body. Your fingers in my hair." He inhales deeply, his hands slipping down my body, resting on my hips. When he pulls back slightly, his dark eyes lock on mine. For a moment, I'm lost in them. In the pools of darkness behind his thick lashes, in his minty scent, in his touch.

But then, just like that, a switch flips.

I practically jump away from him, swatting his chest. "If I didn't know any better, I'd say you were delusional."

I'm fooling a grand total of no one, and we both know it. My voice is shaking, my skin lined with goose bumps. He smiles without missing a beat, lifts a loose fist, and brushes it across my cheek.

"Tell that to the flush on your skin." His knuckle trails to my neck. "Don't worry, Tex. I think about it, too.

Difference is, I don't have to wonder. I *know* you chose the wrong one."

"You are such a jerk." I groan, turning away. "Maybe I won't talk to Lowell after all if this is how you're going to be."

"Probably best. It would be too hard, really, the two of us under one roof. It's inevitable what would happen."

"You either think a lot of yourself or very little of me."

He's still for a moment, then cracks a grin and leans his chest closer to mine, waving a hand in an upward circular motion in front of his chest as if wafting a scent.

My blood runs cold. "What are you doing?"

"Oh, I was just making sure you got enough of a whiff to get you through the rest of the day."

Every nerve ending in my body explodes, my brain short-circuiting. "What did you say?"

His expression is smug and satisfied. It's obviously the exact reaction he was hoping to get from me. "Don't worry about it, Tex. It's natural. Nothing to be ashamed of."

"I have no idea what you're talking about."

He steps back, walking toward the bed again. "It's fine. Your secret's safe with me."

"Stop it, Dallas. I don't have a secret."

"Could've *fooled* me." He runs a hand up his thigh slowly, dragging out the words, then turns to grab something else from his shelf.

My ears are on fire, my pulse pounding in my temples. "You were watching me?"

"I wasn't watching you. I may have come back for my

book, but you seemed a little"—he clears his throat—"*preoccupied*, so I left."

"It wasn't what it looked like, okay? Whatever you think you saw..."

"Oh, I know what I saw." He rubs a hand over his mouth, swiping away a smile. "And don't worry. I came upstairs and made sure we were even."

I shake my head. "I'm going to pretend you didn't say that. And that this entire conversation didn't happen. I'm clearly losing my mind." My eyes widen. "You didn't mention it to Lowell, did you?"

That actually makes him laugh. "You think I'm sharing that with him? You forget I grew up with my brother. He may not look like it, but he packs a mean left hook. I once had a dislocated jaw to prove it." He taps his cheek. "Besides, I haven't talked to him since the little family meeting this morning. He's been out all day."

"Out? Out where?" Lowell didn't mention leaving.

"Just out. He didn't say where he was going. Your friend's gone too, actually." He holds up two fingers, counting, then pats them together like scissors. "Hmm. Both of them. Odd coincidence, wouldn't you say?"

"Are they together?"

"Don't know, didn't ask, don't care." He waves a hand casually. "But, if you need someone to, you know"—his gaze rakes over me—"*help you out* so you don't have to go solo this time, just say the word. I'm here. Well, at least for today."

I storm from the room, refusing to say another word to him, and head straight for Emily's door.

I knock twice, knowing she'll be there. Knowing Dallas has to be lying. But when she doesn't answer, a ball of dread fills my chest.

It can't be true, but it is.

When I push open her door, I find the room empty.

She's gone, and I now know he wasn't lying about Lowell either.

When I turn around, he's lingering in his doorway with a look that says, *I told you so.*

I can't think about that, though. Or about anything else that just happened.

Lowell and Emily are both gone.

What are the odds?

CHAPTER TWENTY-FIVE

CELINE'S JOURNAL

It's been a while, diary. A whole year has come and gone. The weather is changing here. The leaves are turning brown and days are getting shorter.

It seems like everything is dying off, including the perfect life I've had over these past few months.

Simon and I have fallen hard and fast for each other. It's better than the movies because it's real. When we're together...sometimes I think my heart is going to explode from happiness. He's taught me so much. About myself. About life. About growing up.

I'm a different person now. Truly.

I understand things better, you know?

He's shown me a whole new world I didn't know existed. He takes me to fancy restaurants and lets me order anything I like. Oysters, lobster, even wine. No one bats an eye.

He has the most fancy cars I've ever seen and is teaching me to drive them.

He treats me like an adult, not a child. I'm a few years younger than him, but it doesn't feel like it. He doesn't act like it. He worships me in every way. He'd do anything for me. It's like those books Grandma reads. The love and the passion... It's so real and so amazing I can't even explain it.

I never thought I could feel this way.

He's a dream come true.

Sometimes, I swear I think we're the same person, diary. We're so alike. We love all the same things. We laugh at the same jokes. He loves scary movies, just like I do. And the same music I do.

He's my best friend. AND THE BEST KISSER!

When he smiles at me, it's like...it's like he's everything I've ever hoped for.

He calls me CeCe and tells me I'm the woman of his dreams. That I make him laugh like no one ever has. That I make him feel free.

He's beautiful. God, he's beautiful. The dimples in his cheeks, the dark hair across his chest. The dark hair... everywhere.

I can't stop thinking about him.

Dreaming about him.

The moment I turn eighteen next year, we're going to get married. He'll divorce Mrs. Bass, and then it will just be us. Forever.

I'm going to love him for the rest of my life.

CHAPTER TWENTY-SIX

CELINE'S JOURNAL

Everything is ruined.

Mrs. Bass caught us together. She was supposed to be in New York for a few days, and Simon gave my parents the weekend off, bought them tickets to a show in the city, so they were out of the house for the evening. It was the most romantic night—with rose petals all over his bed and champagne, all set up for me.

We had dinner in bed first, with candles and music. We dressed in fluffy robes, like they do in the movies, and just talked and talked. It was the first time we've been able to be together at home without the pressure or worry of someone walking in or catching us.

He kissed me like I was the only thing keeping him alive.

Sometimes, I feel like he might be what's keeping me alive.

When he undressed me, I thought my heart might explode. I feel like we're made for each other. I can't imagine ever being with anyone else. Judy is having sex with Scotty Pearson, but the way she describes it isn't anything like this.

I'm not sure she even likes it that much.

I wish I could tell her about us.

Anyway, we were right in the middle of...it... when the bedroom door flung open. He jumped off of me, threw the covers over my body, and started lying immediately.

"This isn't what it looks like. I'm so sorry. I didn't expect it to happen."

He was crying. Naked on the bedroom floor. Groveling at her feet while I stayed hidden in their bed with no idea what to do. I've never been so embarrassed and hurt and scared. Finally, she stormed past him and ripped the covers off of me.

He did nothing.

She threw the robe I'd been wearing at me and told me to get out.

He watched as I walked away.

I couldn't look at either one of them. I was sure I was going to cry if I did. Once I had the robe on, a robe with her initials on it, I ran out in the hallway, up the stairs, and straight to my room.

I didn't hear from either of them all night. I kept waiting for him to come to my room like he usually does once she falls asleep, but he didn't. If he kissed her, diary, I'm not sure I can stand it.

I want to kill her.

She doesn't deserve him.

No one deserves him but me.

This morning, they were both at my door. They asked me to come across the hall with them, so they could talk to my parents. I was terrified. I just knew my parents would be so furious. They'd never understand. No one understands.

The whole time, Simon wouldn't even look at me. He stayed with her, their hands locked together while my body ached from our time together.

In my parents' room, Mrs. Bass and Simon sat down with my parents, but when she opened her mouth, what she said wasn't what I expected.

"We're going to have to let you go. Effective immediately."

WHAT?!

There was no explanation other than that they were doing some "restructuring," and their positions were no longer needed. After they told *them that, they walked out of the room and left me to face my family.*

They aren't stupid. I know they know something must've happened, but they don't know what. They can't.

To them, I'm still their little baby.

But I know the truth, which is this: their little baby is having one of her own.

CHAPTER TWENTY-SEVEN

CELINE'S JOURNAL

I have to write this quickly. I can't take this journal with me. If my parents ever found it, it would be the end of the world. I can't bear for them to know I'm the reason they've lost their jobs. I can't risk throwing it away either. Someone here might find it and read it.

So, it's going back into my hiding spot until I come back. And I will. This will not be my last day at The Pond.

This is my home. It's where I'm meant to raise my baby. Where I'm meant to grow old with the love of my life.

He still wants me. That much I know.

Simon came to see me while I was packing my things. He didn't have much time, but he asked me to come back to see him on Sunday afternoon. Mrs. Bass will be out of the house for a luncheon, and we'll be able to talk. Three days feels like a lifetime, but I don't have any other choices.

He didn't say he was sorry, but I could see it in his eyes.

He asked me to trust him, but I never stopped.

On Sunday, I'm going to tell him about the baby. We'll have to go to the doctor to confirm, but I'm two months late and I've never missed my time of the month since I started three years ago. Mom says a woman just knows, and I feel like I know. If he loves me like he says he does, he'll leave Sophia and we'll get married like we planned. If he lied, I'm not sure what I'll do. I can't do this on my own. I need him.

Mom and Dad still don't know.

They're going to kill me...

But I've made up my mind, and all I can hope for is that he is still the man I thought he was.

Wish me luck.

CHAPTER TWENTY-EIGHT

AUSTYN

I flip to the next page and then the next. And the next.

They're all blank.

There's nothing else.

This was Celine's final entry.

I flew through them, partially in anger over Lowell not answering my calls and partially because I couldn't stop reading. It's all so scandalous, I keep having to remind myself she was real. That I have her actual hairbrush hidden underneath the dresser in my closet. That the stories I'm reading actually happened in this very house—Simon and Celine slept together in Lowell's parents' room. Maybe in their bed. She came back to this house to tell him about the baby.

And then what happened?

Is that when he killed her? Or was it Sophia who took on that task?

And, more importantly, what do I do with all that I've learned? With all I still have to learn? It's easy to feel trapped in this house, though I know in reality I'm not. I don't have a way to leave without a driver, who would most certainly tell Lowell where I'm going.

A fresh idea hits me. Thinking quickly, I pull out my phone and open my rideshare app. I'm not helpless and I won't pretend to be. Lowell didn't bother telling me he was leaving, nor did Emily. Why should I tell either of them?

I flip to one of the first entries in the journal and pull out the letter from her grandmother. There, in the return address space, is the address where Dorothy Mason lived. If I'm right, it should be the same address where Celine mentioned living with her.

It's a long shot, I realize, but no one here will give me answers, so I'll have to find them myself.

TWO HOURS LATER, I'm pulling up at an address a town over. The houses are smaller and run down, shingles missing from most of the roofs, trash littering the street.

The driver pulls over against the curb, and I begin questioning my decision. If this isn't the right house, or if the people who live here aren't able to help me, I'm going to be stuck here waiting for another driver to pick me up.

"Um, would you mind waiting here?"

The man—middle-aged and weary looking—glances over his shoulder at me. "You only requested a drop-off."

"I know. I just...I'm not sure how this is going to go.

Would you mind waiting for just a few minutes?" I pull my wallet from my purse and hold out a twenty-dollar bill. "I'll tip in the app too, but you can have this if you wait, and"—I riffle through my cash—"I have forty more when I get back."

He contemplates. "How long will you be?"

"Ten, twenty minutes, maybe. You'll be able to see me, I think. I don't plan to go inside."

He's quiet for a moment, eyeing the house, then nods. "Twenty minutes, then I'm calling you to see if I still need to wait. If you don't answer, I'll leave."

"Thank you." I push open the door and step outside into the blistering wind. My hands are like ice—both from the temperature and from my frayed nerves—as I approach the house.

It's a small, one-story home with blue shutters and a metal bumblebee garden stake next to the concrete steps. I climb them—one, two, three—and find myself on the small, concrete front porch.

A lump forms in my throat, thick and suffocating, as I reach for the white lighted doorbell. I press my forefinger into it gently, then drag it back and shove both hands into my pockets.

I practice smiles and greetings in my head as I stand there. This could be the wrong house, I know. They could've sold it years ago. The grandmother could've died while they still lived at The Pond, forcing them to sell the house.

This could've all been a waste of time.

It feels like my last hope, and that scares me.

To be honest, I don't know why I care so much. I don't know Celine. I don't owe her anything. But, once upon a time, I was Celine. Just like every young girl is. Too young to understand the world, too in love to care. Simon took advantage of her, and if it were me, if it were my daughter, I have to hope that someone would care enough to find out what happened to us.

When the door swings open, a young woman stands in front of me. She's beautiful, with creamy, pale skin, dark-brown eyes, and darker hair pulled back into a loose ponytail. Strands of wispy hair frame her face, blowing this way and that in the wind.

She stares at me with a wary expression. "Can I help you?"

"I-I hope so. My name is Austyn Murphy. I... This is going to sound crazy. I'm looking for someone who has information about a young woman named Celine Mason."

A hint of recognition flickers across her face. "Celine Mason? I...I recognize the name, but I don't know anything about her." Her expression wrinkles. "She's been gone for years. What's this about?"

"Is she a relative of yours?" My eyes flick up to the house. "This was her last known address." I wince. "I'm so sorry. I realize how strange this is. I'm...I was recently at a funeral and saw her headstone. It sounds so silly, but I feel...drawn to her. She was so young. Do you have any idea what happened to her?"

I don't think she believes me, but she doesn't say as much. Instead, she folds her arm across her chest. "She was my great-aunt, I think? My grandmother's older sister. Celine was gone before I was born, and my grandmother didn't talk about her often. She was just a baby when Celine died."

"I'm so sorry," I say. It feels like the right thing to say, though her expression clearly says she doesn't need an apology.

"It was a long time ago, like I said. What did you say your name was again? Are you some sort of reporter?"

"I'm Austyn Murphy. And no, I'm not a reporter. I actually own a bakery in Nashville, Tennessee. I'm just here visiting a friend for a funeral." I'm not sure why I lie, but it feels right. For all I know, she may hate the Bass family.

She's quiet for a moment but eventually says, "Sorry, was there something else I could do for you or..."

"No, I just..." I glance back, checking to be sure my driver hasn't abandoned me, should this start going south. "Is there anything else you could tell me about her?"

"Why?" Her nose wrinkles. "This all seems kind of...silly."

"I know. You're right. I'd just like to know what happened to her. No one seems to know, and I just get the feeling there's more to it."

"There was an accident. She was in the car with her boss or...something like that." She shakes her head. "It's no real mystery."

"Her boss? Do you mean Simon Bass?"

"I'm really not sure. Her boss. That's all I remember my grandma saying." From inside the house, I hear the sounds of a baby crying. She glances behind her. "My son's just waking up. I'm sorry, but I should go."

The last bit of hope drains from my system, and I look away, feeling defeated. "Well, thank you for your time. Would it be okay to leave my number? Maybe if you think of anything else, you could call or text me?"

She chews her bottom lip for a second, then puts up a finger. "Wait here just a sec, okay?"

"Sure."

She disappears behind the closing door, and within minutes, the baby's cries settle down. Turning to face the driver, I give him a thumbs-up I hope he'll take to mean things are going well. I drag my jacket sleeves down over my hands, trying to warm up.

Several minutes pass, to where I'm wondering if she's just going to leave me standing here and never return, but finally, the door swings open again.

"Here. I have this. I'm not sure if this will help, but" —she holds out a slip of paper—"you're welcome to have it, if so. It was in an old photo album. She was...around fourteen or fifteen there, I think."

Realizing it's a photograph rather than a slip of paper, I flip it over in my hands. In black and white, a young Celine Mason stares up at me. She's not at all what I pictured. Her ivory skin and long dark hair are a stark contrast. She's sitting on these very porch steps next to a man and a woman, and I can't help noticing she favors the man much more. Her mother and father, I suspect. Her smile is soft and childlike. Innocent. She has no idea what will happen to her just a few years later.

"It's all I have of her, really. I'm sorry I can't be of much help."

"No, this is perfect. Thank you. I really appreciate it."

Her lips dip inward with an awkward smile, and she steps back inside without agreeing to take my number. I don't bother asking again as I stare down at the picture. Eventually, I make my way back to the car. It's more than I expected, and yet, it still doesn't help me much at all, but at least it's something. If nothing else, at least someone is remembering Celine. At least someone has heard her story.

Back in the car, I give the driver the next address and pass him two more twenty-dollar bills. "Thank you again for waiting."

I'm quiet on the way to the Bass Industries office, trying to decide what I'll say to Lowell. It's nearly an hour before we arrive and I get out of the car, the cold air slamming into me once again.

I thought California was supposed to be warm.

"Thank you again," I say, sending the rest of his tip through my phone and waving as I walk up the stairs and into the building. On my way, I send Lowell a quick text.

> Hey, I'm going to stop by your office. I'll hang out for the next few hours and we can go to dinner from there.

Maybe I'm just trying to avoid Dallas at this point. I'm not entirely sure. I search the board on the right side of the room for Lowell's name and find his father's instead. They haven't changed it yet.

John Bass, CEO

He's on the top floor. I step into the elevator and press the button. My body tingles with nerves, hoping he'll be okay with the surprise visit. Hoping he'll be receptive to my talk with him about letting Dallas stay a while longer.

It may be a mistake, but it feels like the right thing to do. I'm just going to have to control myself. For goodness' sake, I'm a woman, not a hormone-ridden teenager. And Dallas is just a man. An annoyingly cocky man.

Lowell's reply comes through just as the doors open.

Sorry, babe. I'm swamped right now. Don't bother coming. I won't be much of a host. I'll stop by the house for you as soon as I can.

My heart drops as I read the message then and drops again when I look up and my gaze lands on my fiancé through the glass walls of his office. He's smiling, looking decidedly *not swamped*, as he stares at the person sitting across from him.

The *woman* sitting across from him.

Emily.

CHAPTER TWENTY-NINE

I should've stormed into the office and demanded to know what was going on.

I should've called him and told him to look up.

I should've let them both realize I had caught them red-handed.

Instead, I turned and fled like I was the one who had done something wrong.

Now, I'm back at The Pond. I'm not sure what to do with myself. Anger comes in waves—anger at myself, at Lowell, at Emily. Anger for letting myself get so wrapped up in this Celine thing that I haven't seen what's clearly right in front of me. I just bought his lies. Ate them up like I was a sad, starving puppy.

I'm embarrassed by how blind I've been. How foolish.

I invited her here. And I knew—*I knew*—that something wasn't right. I've felt it in my gut since that first night. And when I saw her name in his ledger... When I saw the payments going through each month, how could I have been so stupid?

I stare down into the mug of tea I'm drinking, letting out a huff.

"Hey, do you care if I take Dad's—" Dallas's words drop off when he sees me. "Sorry, I thought you were Fallon." His expression goes limp. "You okay?"

"Mm-hmm."

He approaches the table, slipping into the chair in front of me. "You don't *look* okay." He folds his hands together, waiting.

"Are Lowell and Emily having an affair?"

He's still for a moment. "Do you think they're having an affair?"

"Yes." I don't even consider lying as the word slips out. "I don't know why it's taken me so long to realize it."

"Maybe because you didn't want it to be true."

I inhale sharply, fighting back against the tears I feel stinging my eyes. "So, it is true, then?"

He looks down at his hands. "I don't have any proof other than a gut instinct. If I did, I would've told you."

"Why?"

The question brings his eyes back to meet mine. "*Why* what?"

"Why would you have told me? I'm nothing to you. He's your brother. For all I know, you'd protect him. You could be lying to me right now."

"Why would I lie to you? You really think I want to protect him?"

"Bass protect their own." My voice is so dry I hardly recognize it.

"Yeah, well, sometimes they don't." He leans back in his chair. "You know, I'm not him, Austyn. I'm not anything like him."

"Meaning what?"

"I guess you'll have to figure it out."

I drop my head into my hands, whining, "I don't need anything else to figure out."

"Look, just talk to Lowell, okay? Or, better yet, talk to Emily. She's your friend, isn't she? Why don't you ask her?"

"You told me not to trust anyone, remember?"

"I didn't say trust them, I just said ask them."

"Well, I *have* asked him. He said it's not true, of course. I found payments he was making to her, and I let him convince me they were payments to a cleaner with the same name."

"*What?*"

I drop my head into my hands, my voice echoing in my palms. "I've just been so distracted trying to find out what happened to Celine, I—" I stop talking, realizing what I've said. When I look up, Dallas's face has paled.

"What do you mean *what happened to her?*"

"Who was she, Dallas? Why did you tell me to lie to Lowell about her?"

He presses his lips together, looking away.

"I know she died."

"Well, obviously. Hence the whole gravestone thing."

"I know she died here when she was just seventeen. I know she was with your grandfather when it happened."

He stands. "Come with me." He doesn't wait to see if I'll follow, but I do. I follow him out of the room, up the stairs, and into his bedroom. When he shuts the door, his voice is low. "You shouldn't talk about that here. People are always listening."

"What people? The staff? Why would they care?"

"They're loyal to the Bass family, Austyn. Unflinchingly loyal. *Jump in front of a bus, lie to the cops, kill their own family for us,* loyal. Most of them have been in his house, in this family, longer than I've been alive. My dad used to explain it like everyone in this house is part of this...this cell, right? Like we're all a part of this thing and we all have our jobs to do and roles to play, but at the end of the day, everyone answers to one person and one person only. Now, that person is Lowell."

"But what does Lowell have to do with Celine? She would've been dead long before he was ever born."

He presses his lips together, shaking his head. "You don't understand. Families don't get rich like this, strong like this, without blood on their hands—literally and figuratively. They don't get by without their fair share of secrets. Celine is a secret that's been passed down. She's a secret that everyone in this house will kill to protect, Lowell included."

"You're being ridiculous." I scoff. "He may be cheating on me, but he would never hurt me. Not physically."

He shrugs one shoulder. "Like you said, Bass protect Bass. You aren't a Bass yet."

"And how do I know you aren't protecting him right now somehow? How do I know you won't hurt me?"

"How do you know I won't..." His voice fades, sadness filling his eyes. "I couldn't, Austyn. You have to realize that."

"Why not?"

"I don't know, okay?" His hands fly to either side of his head. "I don't fucking know. Believe me, if I did, I'd be a lot better off. If I could just be more like them. Like him."

"Like him, how?"

"Bass are supposed to be able to shut down all emotion when it comes to making decisions. Always the head, never the..."

"Heart?" I offer.

He scowls. "Jesus. I'm not a Girl Scout. I'm just saying... I'm not... I don't have whatever it is they have that allows them to do whatever it takes to win or get ahead or whatever. It's just never been that important to me." He gestures to the boxes resting on his bed. "I guess that's why he gets the house and I'm on my way out, hmm?"

"But I don't understand... Do you know what happened to Celine?"

"Not fully, no. And, even if I did, you could never know."

"Why not?"

"Because that would put you in danger, and I can't..."

It's as if he's so full of words he can't seem to choose what to say next. His entire body looks ready to burst. "I can't... do that...to you."

I soften at his words. They're kind, even if they're also terrifying. "You're scaring me, Dallas."

"Good." He shoves his hands into his pockets. "Being scared will keep you alive."

"Are you actually saying he'd hurt me? Seriously?"

"If you came between him and what he wants... without a doubt. Without a moment's hesitation. It's who he is."

I swallow. "So, what do I do with that?"

"You can't do anything right now. You just need to play it cool. Stop asking about Celine. Focus on making him think everything's okay. And then, when you have the chance, if you trust me, I would run. As far away and as fast as you can."

"He knows where I live."

"He's not going to chase you, Austyn. He can't let himself look weak. If you just leave him without letting on there's any other reason, if he doesn't think you're a threat to the family, he'll move on. And you'll be safe."

His words weigh on me.

I'm not safe here.

I'm not safe with the man I love.

How can any of that be true?

I've known Lowell for years. Loved him for years. I just met Dallas days ago.

Why would I take his word over Lowell's?

Then again, ever since we arrived at The Pond, Lowell has changed. He's lying to me.

For some reason, I don't think Dallas is.

Dallas's lips upturn with a wry grin, but it feels empty. Sad. "I told you you chose the wrong brother."

CHAPTER THIRTY

Lowell arrives home around six, by which time I've had a bath, fixed my hair, applied my makeup, and gotten dressed. Emily came back a few hours earlier, but when she knocked on my bedroom door, I told her I was getting ready and didn't have time to hang out.

There was no hint of guilt in her eyes. No clues that she was lying when she said she'd gone out for coffee and decided to do some shopping again.

Why am I so easy to lie to?

I wanted to scream, to kick her out, to demand the truth, but I had Dallas's advice ringing in my ears. For all I know, he's lying to me, too, but it's all I have.

Now, I'm in the back of the town car, Lowell's warm and soapy scent all around me, his hand locked with mine as he tells me all about his day at the new office.

Funnily enough, there's an Emily-shaped hole in his story that I can't yet bring up.

At the restaurant, we take our seats and Lowell orders us a bottle of wine.

Once the waiter has filled our glasses and taken our orders, he finally clears his throat. "You've been quiet tonight. I feel like I'm the only one talking."

"I've just...got a lot on my mind, I guess." I shrug.

"Want to talk about it?"

No, because I'm scared to know if it's true. I can't say that, though. I have to be a grown-up. Have to deal with this.

"I came by your office today."

He opens his mouth, prepared to respond, then closes it again. "Y-you did?" His hand flies to his tie, and he adjusts it, then tugs on the collar of his suit jacket. "When?"

"When I texted you to say I was coming."

"You didn't come up." He's keeping his voice low.

I blink. "I did."

"You did? Henry didn't tell me you'd left the house. I never saw you."

"You were busy, remember?"

We stare at each other for several seconds, both waiting to see who's going to crack first.

It's Lowell who does. He steadies himself, both hands flat on the linen tablecloth. "You should've come in if you were already there."

Apparently, I'm going to have to spell this out for him. "I came upstairs right as I got your text about how busy you were. And when I got to your office, Emily was there."

"Yeah, she was... I assumed she told you she was coming."

I tilt my head to the side, waiting for him to go on.

"She was probably embarrassed, but she came by to ask if she was causing problems between us. I guess she can sense some of the tension. It was a surprise to me. I hadn't expected her to be there."

"Why wouldn't she just come to me and ask? Why go to you?"

"I don't know. I guess she thought you might lie to her, being friends and all. That you wouldn't want to hurt her feelings." He pauses, then adds urgently, "Don't worry. I told her she's not causing any problems. That she's welcome to stay as long as she likes." His lips press together.

"Okay, then why didn't you tell me?"

"I didn't want to cause more stress. I cleared the air with her and told her everything was fine. It was done. Over. I was trying to do what I thought was best. The last thing Emily wants is to cause issues for us, Austyn. She loves you. We both do."

I'm dumbfounded. I should've known this was how it was going to go. Of course, he has a perfectly reasonable explanation for why they were there, why they were together behind my back, just like he has a reasonable explanation for everything else.

"Fine, but that's still no reason to lie and say you were busy."

"Well, I *was* busy. It was my first day back in the office—not to mention my first day in a brand-new office

—and we had a client who wanted to meet in person. I was trying to get things straightened up, get settled in before he arrived. Emily didn't give me a heads-up that she was coming or I would've told her I was in the middle of something, too. It didn't seem polite to kick her out once she was already at the door."

I nod. "Okay."

His laugh is patronizing; my blood boils at the sound of it. "What did you think was happening, exactly? You've got to get this *affair* thing out of your head, sweetheart." He dips his head forward slightly, running his tongue over his bottom lip. "I think I have just the thing to help with that." His hands slide across the tablecloth, reaching for mine, and I'm too slow at moving them away.

"I want to set a date for the wedding. I was thinking Valentine's Day."

The words take my breath away. He can't be serious. "Valentine's Day is in a month, Lowell. We can't get married in a month."

"Why can't we?"

Because your brother has me convinced you might try to kill me.

Because you might be sleeping with my best friend.

Because I think you might be hiding things from me.

Because I'm not sure I trust you anymore.

Because I don't want to stay here.

Because I'm afraid to tell you that.

Those are all the things I want to say to him. Instead, I hear myself saying, "Because there's way too much to do before then."

"So? Make a list, we'll get it done—"

"It's not that simple. There are dresses that have to be ordered and may take months to get alterations. The cake, the flowers, the venue... Places book out years in advance sometimes."

"Well, we could have it at The Pond. Or, if you'd rather have it somewhere else, I'll make it happen. Name the place and I'll book it. Any place you want. I'll offer five times what they're booking for. And same for the dresses. Fallon can design them all, and we'll cover whatever rush fees she needs to make it happen, whatever it takes. I thought you would want to make our cake, but if not, we can hire someone for that, too. If they're booked up, we'll buy out their entire list. All their time from here until the wedding. You can have one hundred cakes if you want. And, as for everything else, I can hire someone whose full-time job is just to plan the wedding. I'm not trying to add any extra stress on you. I just want you to be my wife. I'm ready for you to be my wife." He squeezes my hands, his thumbs rubbing over my knuckles in slow circles.

"I don't know what to say, Lowell, I—"

"Then say yes." He nods, coaxing me. "Say yes, and let's celebrate."

The waiter approaches with our plates, setting them in front of us while Lowell's eyes remain locked on me expectantly.

"Okay," I squeak, finally. "Yes."

He stands abruptly, leaning forward to kiss my lips over the table. I want to be happy, to feel the joy I see written on his face. I want to believe everything he's told me. Every explanation he's given. They make sense, they really do.

I want to go back to being happy. To settle into my new life. To feel safe again.

Problem is, I'm not sure I can.

CHAPTER THIRTY-ONE

I'm coming out of the bathroom the next morning, still dressed in pajamas with my hair wet from my shower, when there's a knock on the door.

When I open it, I find Emily standing in the hallway. For the first time since her arrival, she's dressed down in a sweatshirt and yoga pants with no makeup. Her long blonde hair is pulled back in a loose ponytail.

"Are you busy?" Her voice is weak. It looks like she's been crying.

"I'm...no." I step back, letting her in the room, and she sits down. "Are you all right?"

"I'm okay." She eases down onto the upholstered ivory bedroom bench at the end of our bed. "Did you guys have fun last night?"

"We did." I nod. "We're...uh, we're picking a date. For the wedding." I clasp my hands together in front of my stomach, trying to get a read on her expression.

She seems solemn. Lifeless. Exhausted. I see no flicker of anger or jealousy in her eyes. "Oh. You are?"

"Yes. Lowell is thinking about Valentine's Day."

"That's..." She sighs. "That's very soon."

"Are you sure you're okay? You don't look well." I move to sit down next to her.

Her next words send a wave of shock through my body. "I need to tell you something."

This is it. This is what I've been preparing for.

"Okay."

"Austyn, I'm... I'm pregnant." Her hands move to cradle her stomach, and as she says it, the hazel of her eyes is flooded with tears.

The room around me goes silent and blurry, as if I'm passed out but still fully conscious. I can't breathe. Can't think. It isn't possible. It can't be true.

"Pregnant?" I hear myself saying. It doesn't even sound like my voice.

"It's very early." A tear slips down her cheek. "I just found out."

"Whose baby is it?" I can't stop the question from leaving my mouth.

She glances down, sniffling. "Just some guy. We met in a bar right after Grayson told me he wanted a divorce."

Some guy. That's her excuse.

Suddenly it hits me: that's why she went to see Lowell yesterday. To tell him about the baby.

His baby.

I feel like I'm going to be sick.

"Have you told him?"

When she looks back up at me, there's shame evident in her eyes. "I'm not going to. I don't want his help with this. He's no one." Her hand trembles as she reaches for the collar of her shirt, tugging on it.

"Fair enough. Have you...made an appointment? Do you want me to go with you?"

She pinches the bridge of her nose with her finger and thumb. "Not yet. I have no idea what I'm going to do."

My insides are at war. On the one hand, I want to be there for my friend. If this were under any other circumstances, I would've already gathered her into a hug and tried to soothe her. But, as I'm fairly certain the baby is Lowell's, I'm actively trying to stop myself from falling apart.

"Have you... Have you told anyone else?"

She shakes her head, tears staining her cheeks again. Her chin quivers as she answers. "Who would I tell? You're all I have."

"Is there...any chance it could be Grayson's? Would he want to know? Would this change anything?"

Her shoulders shake with sobs. "No. I don't think it would change anything."

She hasn't said it couldn't be his, so I lean into that. "Maybe you should call and talk to him. Explain everything. He still cares about you, Em. He has to."

She sniffles, shaking her head. "Yeah, maybe."

Another knock on the door interrupts us. "Are you ready?" We both look up to see Fallon standing in the half-open doorway. Her grin falls the second she sees us.

"I'm sorry. Am I interrupting?"

"It's fine," Emily says, standing and wiping her tears.

"Wait, Em, we aren't done." I try to stop her, but she's already reaching for the door.

She swings it open and looks back at me over her shoulder. "It's okay. I'm not feeling well anyway. I should lie down. We'll see each other later, okay?"

She slips past Fallon and crosses the hall without looking back. Once her door has shut, Fallon eyes me. "You're not wearing that, are you?"

"What do you mean?" I stare down at myself. "Wearing this for what?"

"Dress shopping!" She beams. "Lowell told me you guys are trying to get a jump on everything and asked me to come over and take you to try some things on so we can start planning. Now, obviously, we're going to want something custom for you, but I thought if you could give me some direction as to what you like—as in material, cut, style, etc.—I could do a few mock-ups for you before we get the order put in. Valentine's Day is cutting it, but we'll make it happen. Oh, and I'll get your measurements today, too. We can get Emily's later—I'm assuming she'll be a bridesmaid—and I already have mine, of course. Will the girls be flower girls? We can design their little dresses to match yours. Lowell's never said if you have little cousins or nieces you'd be using instead. No pressure, of course."

Her eyes dart back and forth between mine, obviously waiting for me to answer or address one of the million questions she's just thrown my way. "Well, come on. What are you waiting for? Get dressed already. I'll wait downstairs. Don't take long, though. I've had Martin leave the car running."

"Fallon, I—I had no idea any of this was happening."

"Lowell didn't tell you?"

"No, he didn't. And it's really very sweet of you to offer, but I have work stuff I was planning to do today."

"Work? What, your little bakery thing? Lowell said you were hiring someone else to handle that."

I clench my jaw. "I have no plans to do that just yet."

How dare he?

"Oh. Well..." She clicks her tongue. "Can't you just do it this afternoon when we get back? I mean, we are on a *bit* of a time crunch, after all."

"Right. Okay." *Grin and bear it.* "Well, just let me get changed, then, and blow-dry my hair. I'll be right down."

She grins, blowing air kisses my way. "Can't wait! This will be so fun!"

TWO HOURS LATER, we pull up in front of a bridal shop downtown. The driver stops in front of the building and lets us out, obviously showing no regard for stopping two lanes of traffic to do so.

Fallon leads the way, her heels clicking loudly as we cross the sidewalk. Before we go in, she pauses and turns to face me.

"Look, I've been meaning to apologize if I haven't been the kindest person since you arrived. I really wanted to be better at this, but it's all been really stressful, and I know I haven't handled it well."

I'm taken aback by the apology and the sincerity with which she says it.

"It's okay—"

"It's not. That night when I said you didn't belong in the room when we were discussing the will, when I compared you to the staff, I didn't mean it. I was just..." She looks down, searching for the word.

"You were just grieving," I fill in for her. "I know. It's okay, I promise."

Seeming satisfied, she pulls open the door and produces a notebook from her purse, clicking her pen. "After you."

The store walls are a light pink, the carpets plush white. The air smells of flowers, and even under the bright-white studio lights, they've somehow made it feel cozy with racks and racks of bridal gowns, a wall of individual changing rooms hidden behind champagne-colored curtains, and a long, golden sofa in the center of the room.

"Hello, hello!" A cheerful woman who looks to be in her midfifties rushes toward us from somewhere in the back. Her hair is held in place by what must be a full can of hairspray, and the apples of her cheeks are a shade of pink that nearly matches the walls. "You must be Austyn."

She extends a hand to Fallon, who points to me, and the woman's hand quickly shifts. "I'm Cheryl."

I accept the handshake and glance around. "I'm

Austyn, yes. And this is Fallon. Wow. It's beautiful in here."

"Thank you," she says, with a pride that could only belong to the store's owner. "We do everything we can to make this day special for our brides." She glances around. "Is this... I mean, is it just you two?"

"Yes," Fallon says.

My mom should be here. I'm not sure why the thought occurs to me then for the first time, but it does, washing over me. I feel dizzy. Up until this moment, none of it has felt real. I was just playing along. But now... now we're at a real dress shop looking at actual wedding gowns. Am I ready for this? Before our arrival at The Pond, I would've said yes. Now, I'm not sure. "It's only the two of us, and we're just looking."

"Of course. Of course. Why don't you two look through the racks while I get us some champagne, okay?"

She walks away, her hips swaying as if she were on a runway.

"Okay, do you have any idea what style you like?" Fallon pulls me to a rack, holding out dresses for my opinion. She forces me to feel fabrics and give my thoughts on them. I mostly nod. I should have opinions on this, but I don't. All I can think of is the fact that my mom should be here and my best friend should most certainly not be pregnant with my fiancé's baby.

"You okay?" Fallon asks after a while.

"Just distracted. Sorry."

"It's a lot." Her voice is kinder than I expected. She says it with the sincerity of someone who truly gets it, suddenly reminding me of the Fallon I met when we first arrived at The Pond. "Planning a wedding so quickly, marrying into our crazy family." Her smile is soft as she pulls out another dress, and I shake my head. She jots something else down in her notebook.

"It *is* a lot." My voice cracks as the words leave my mouth, and her smile fades away. "Not because you're crazy, just because...it all feels like it's happening so fast. I mean, we've been dating for, like, seven years, so it's not fast. But two weeks ago, I hadn't even met you guys, and now, I'm living in your family's house, supposed to be giving up the bakery I put my life's work into, and we're getting married in a month."

"Have you told that to my brother? I'm sure he'd be okay with waiting if you need more time."

"I love Lowell," I whisper. "I want to marry him." It's not a lie. I know that much in my gut. But there's so much I can't say.

"Why do I sense there's a *but* coming?"

"I'm just...a little overwhelmed, I think."

"That's understandable." She picks up the champagne Cheryl brought over and takes a sip. "That's all a *little* overwhelming."

"I always thought my mom would be here for this."

"Do you want her to be? Lowell said you wouldn't mind if it was just the two of us since we're so short on time, but if you want, we could send the jet for her and do this tomorrow instead. I mean, we're not actually buying your dress today, either way, so we'll absolutely have her here when you try on your *actual* dress." She lowers her voice. "Which will be much nicer than any of these."

I chuckle. "Thank you. I'll be okay. She's a social worker, and it's hard for her to take off with short notice."

She's quiet for a while, sifting through dresses again. When she speaks, she's not looking at me. "You know, when we were planning my wedding, my mom drove me crazy. I left her out of as many decisions as I could because of it. But, now that she's gone"—her shoulders rise and fall with a deep breath—"I'm just so glad she was there."

I reach out, placing a careful hand on her shoulder. It feels strange, but when she looks back at me with tears in her eyes, I know it was the right thing to do.

She puts her hand over mine for a brief second, then pats it and swipes her fingers under both eyes. "So, seriously, whatever you need... I'm here. I promised Lowell we'll make it happen."

"Thank you, Fallon."

She bumps my hip with hers, beaming at me. "I told you I've always wanted a sister. There's too much testosterone around here if you ask me."

"Are you very close with your brothers?" I ask.

One shoulder jerks up with a playful shrug. "I mean, what are you going to do, y'know? They're my brothers. They drive me crazy sometimes, but I'm glad I have them. At the end of the day, I love and would kill for them." She studies me. "Do you have siblings?"

"No, it's just me."

"I didn't think so. The way you look when we argue

sometimes... I can tell you aren't used to it. It's just another Tuesday around here, y'know? You haven't seen the worst of it."

My eyes widen.

"Oh, I'm not kidding. There's been blood. And hospital visits." She laughs. "Some days we hate each other, but we're the only ones allowed to say that. It just comes with the territory of siblings."

I smile sadly. Emily was like my sister once, but I don't know what she is to me anymore. I turn my attention to a new dress, running my finger over the lace. "I like this one a lot."

"Noted." She pulls away from me, writing something new down. "Do you know how many bridesmaids you'll have?"

"I hadn't really thought about it." I pull down another dress, but it's too heavy, the skirt too full. "Nothing like this one."

She nods. "Got it. Will...Emily be one?"

Something about the way she asks the question causes me to hesitate. I look at her over my shoulder. "I... I don't know. Probably, I guess. Why do you ask?"

"No reason, really. Just curious." Now it's her turn to busy herself looking through the dresses.

"Is there a reason she shouldn't be?"

She hesitates, then keeps sorting, pushing dresses this way and that. She can't even really be paying attention to what she's looking at. "No, not that I can think of."

"Everything okay over here, girls? Can I help you find anything specific?" Cheryl is back, bringing with her a fresh bottle of champagne and a book of color swatches. I guess they assume plying you with drinks will help loosen your wallet. "Here are the bridesmaids' and mothers' dress color samples. As I told you, we can have any of the designs made in any of these colors, so if you have something in mind, just ask."

"Thank you, Cheryl. We're fine here," Fallon says dismissively, waving her away and refilling both of our glasses.

When we first arrived at The Pond, I would've been bothered by Fallon's treatment of Cheryl, but by now, I'm used to it. Besides, I have bigger things on my plate.

"Emily's pregnant," I say. It's not really my secret to tell, but then again, she didn't ask me to keep it quiet.

Fallon lowers her champagne glass from her lips. "She is?"

"That's what she was telling me this morning."

"Wow. Is she... Is she happy about it?"

"I don't really know. She's going through a lot. I'm sure it's hard."

"Yeah, I'm sure it is." She takes another drink, her eyes locked on the wall behind me, lost in thought. "Does... Does Lowell know?"

A boulder settles in my gut. "I'm not sure. Why?"

Her cheeks pinken, and it's as if she's woken up from a trance. "I was just thinking... Well, someone should tell him so he can inform the chef. You know...wouldn't want to serve anything she shouldn't be eating right now."

"Right." I swallow. "Fallon?"

She meets my eyes.

"Is there something going on with Lowell and Emily?"

The laugh she gives is so over the top, it wouldn't even merit an audition callback for the role of Tree Number Three in a high school drama production. "*What?* Don't be ridiculous."

Her phone rings, its shrill sound interrupting my train of thought. She spins around, reaching for her purse and pulling it out. She stares briefly at the screen with a frown before placing it to her ear.

"Hello?" She forces a fake smile, but it fades away in an instant. "What do you mean?" There's a pause. "How is that possible? I don't understand." Another pause. "Okay. Okay. We'll be right there."

She drops the phone to her side, eyes wide. "We have to go."

"What's wrong?"

Her mouth opens and closes again, eyes still lost to whatever news she's just received. When she meets my gaze, finally, it's with a vacant stare. "Emily's...gone."

CHAPTER THIRTY-TWO

Back at home, the house is pure chaos. Emily's room is filled with people, though none of them are the right people.

Not Emily.

Not the police.

Instead, a team of housekeepers searches the room while Dallas, Lowell, Fallon, and I stand off to one side, arguing about the best course of action.

"We need to call the police," I say for what feels like the hundredth time. No one is listening to me.

"We don't do that," Lowell says again. "We'll handle this on our own."

"Handle what? She's missing. Something might've happened. She wouldn't just leave."

"Are you sure? All her stuff *is* gone," Fallon points out again.

"She wouldn't just leave. She told me this morning she'd see me later."

"Maybe there was a change of plans," Lowell says.

"A change of plans? From what? Living here to suddenly not?"

"Austyn, please." Lowell moves closer to me, putting a hand on my shoulder. It doesn't feel loving or comforting but rather cold and controlling. "You're not helping anything. Why don't you try to call her again?"

Grateful to have a reason to get away from them, I step out of the room and tap her name in my call log, pressing the phone to my ear. It goes to her voice mail instantly.

Her phone is still off.

This isn't like her.

When the line beeps, prompting me to leave a message, I do. "Em, it's...it's me again. Listen, we're really scared, okay? I'm terrified. I know you have a lot going on, but all of your stuff is just gone. If you've left, I'm not mad, but could you just call me back and let me know you're okay? I just want to be sure you're okay. Um...bye. Call me."

I end the call, tears stinging my cheeks. I move farther down the stairs to the first floor, scrolling through my phone's call log again. I land on my mom's name, the only person I want to talk to right now, and click it.

She answers on the second ring. "Hello?"

"Hey, Momma."

I can hear the worry in her voice. "Austyn? What's wrong, sweetheart? Are you crying?"

I step into the study, shutting the door behind me. "Everything is so messed up."

"What's messed up, honey? Did something happen with Lowell?"

"No. Yes. I don't know. It's... Do you remember Emily Erikson? She's, well, she's Emily Campbell now. From Vandy?"

"Oh, Emily! Of course. Goodness, I haven't heard you talk about her in years."

"Yeah, it's been a while, but she's here. Or, well, she's been here. She's going through some things with her marriage, and she called the other day to ask if she could stay with us."

"She asked if she could come stay there?"

"Well, *there*, actually. Home. But when I told her we were here in California, Lowell offered for her to come here."

"Well, that was nice of him."

"Yeah, I guess. I mean, yeah, it was, it's just... Well, she's been here a few days, and this morning she told me she'd just found out she's pregnant, and now she's gone."

"Gone? What do you mean?"

"When I left the house this morning, she told me she'd see me later, but Lowell's brother noticed her bedroom door open earlier and all of her stuff was gone. Like she packed and left without telling me."

"Did you two have a fight?"

"No. Things were fine when we talked last."

"Well, honey, she's a grown woman. I'm sure, wherever she is, she's fine. Did you try to call her?"

"Several times."

"What about her husband? What was his name?"

"Grayson." I nod. "Yeah, I didn't think about calling him, but I doubt he'll know where she is. They weren't speaking, as far as I know."

"Things may have changed with her news. Why don't you give him a call and then call me back?"

I approach the bookshelf, running my finger over the dust-free surface. There's certainly something to be said about having a cleaning staff on hand.

"Yeah, okay. I'll do that."

"Okay, honey. Don't cry. I'm sure it'll all be okay."

"Thanks, Mom. I love you." I want to tell her so much more, about my suspicions of their affair and the sudden wedding date, but Emily is my priority for the moment. And, even if she wasn't, I don't want Lowell to overhear.

"I love you too, Austyn."

I end the call and click on my contacts, searching through them. While they were planning the wedding, I had Grayson's number saved in my phone in case there were ever wedding emergencies I didn't want to worry Emily with. Though I rarely had to use it, I've never been more thankful for that foresight.

I spy his name, **Grayson Campbell**, and tap it. The phone rings four times, and I'm sure it's going to go to voice mail just as he picks up.

"Hello?" He sounds just the same.

"Grayson, hey, it's Austyn Murphy—"

"Yeah, I know, Austyn. I still have your number saved. Everything okay?" He sounds tired. Or annoyed, maybe.

"Um, yeah, I was actually hoping you've spoken with Emily."

"Emily?" He says her name as if it's a ridiculous notion. As if I might be talking about another Emily. "Can't say that I have. We're getting divorced, actually. I thought she'd have told you."

"No, uh, she did. She's been... She was staying with me, actually. For the past few days. But I can't find her. You haven't talked to her at all?"

"Not in a week or so, no."

"I'm worried about her, Gray. It's not like her to disappear."

"Not like her? Austyn, you haven't talked to her in, what, two years? How would you know what she's like anymore?" His words are hateful, more than I've ever known him to be. I was always Emily's friend, not his, so maybe this is how it'll be moving forward. "Look," he says, his voice calmer, "I'm sure she'll call you, but in the meantime, it's not...it's not really my problem. She left me. As far as I'm concerned, she can do whatever the hell she pleases."

"Wait, what? *She* left *you?*"

"Don't act so shocked. If she's staying with you, surely she's mentioned that."

"No, she hasn't, actually. She said you left her."

He scoffs. "'Course she did. Leave it to her to make me the bad guy here, too."

"But...she was devastated. She said she loved you and you just sprung it on her."

"Well, she lied, Austyn. Em's been cheating on me

for months now. When I found out, I begged her to end it, and instead, she left me. Said she wanted a divorce and she left. Guess now I know where she's been."

"She was cheating on you? With...with who?"

"No idea. She would never tell me." His tone is clipped. "Listen, I'm gonna go, okay? Don't get yourself too worked up about her. She's not the girl you remember."

"Will you at least call me if you hear from her?"

"Yes, but I won't. Goodbye, Austyn." With that, he ends the call and I'm left staring at the family portraits on the bookshelf. Pictures of Lowell, Dallas, and Fallon growing up, playing sports, graduating. Pictures of ski trips, mountain getaways, and beach vacations. Going to the next shelf, there are photos of their father growing up —I recognize some of the pictures from his memorial video at the funeral. He was always handsome, like Lowell, with kind, mysterious eyes like Dallas.

My eyes flick to the next set of pictures, and I freeze.

"Everything okay in here?" Dallas's voice breaks through the silence, but I'm frozen in place. "Hello? Earth to Austyn." He moves closer, coming up behind me.

When he reaches me, I outstretch a finger, pointing to the black-and-white photograph on the shelf of a young couple holding a baby wrapped in a thick blanket.

"Who is this, Dallas?"

He steps beside me, leaning in closer. "Who?"

"This couple."

"Uh, that's my...grandparents."

"Simon Bass?" I turn my head to look at him.

"Yes, stalker. Why?" His brows draw down.

"It's impossible..."

"What do you mean?"

I shake my head. "Do you know who the woman is with him?"

"Of course. It's my grandmother. Sophia."

My mind is spinning. "None of this makes any sense."

"What are you talking about?"

"That woman." I jab my finger into the glass of the picture frame, my nail touching her chin. "She's not Sophia Bass—"

"Of course she is. I think I'd know—"

"She's Celine Mason. And she should've been dead long before this picture was taken."

CHAPTER THIRTY-THREE

"How could that possibly be Celine Mason?" Dallas asks, jogging to keep up with me.

When we get to the foyer, my purse is missing from where I left it on the sofa table, which means one of the housekeepers must've taken it to my room. I jog up the stairs, stopping long enough to check on Fallon and Lowell, who are still in Emily's room with their backs to me. When I know the coast is clear, I hurry down the hall and slip into my bedroom. Once Dallas is inside, he shuts the door gently.

"How could that possibly be Ce—"

"I heard you." I grab my purse from where it rests on the floor, lift it and place it on the bed. "I know what you said, and I don't have an answer." I spin around with the picture in my hand, panting and out of breath. "But you can't tell me that woman isn't this little girl all grown up. And this little girl...is Celine Mason."

He takes the photograph, staring at it with disbelief.

The closer it gets to his face, the thinner the line of his lips gets.

"This woman—this girl—she's my grandmother. I'm sure of it." He shakes his head, still not looking at me. "Where did you find this?"

"I..." I should come up with a lie, but I'm already trusting him with so much, it seems pointless. "I went to visit Celine's family. They gave it to me. There are others," I add, for good measure.

He looks up, eyes squinted closed, trying to think. "None of this makes any sense. How could Celine also be Sophia? And how the hell do you have their address?"

"I have another confession..." I brace myself. "When I moved in, I found a journal that belonged to Celine Mason."

"You *what*? Where?"

"It's gone. I brought it to her family," I lie. "But first, I read it. That's how I got the address. It was on a letter she'd saved inside."

"What was in it?" His expression is unreadable.

"The journal? It's from the year that Celine lived here. She moved in with her family, but she...she fell in love with Simon—with your grandfather."

His Adam's apple bobs. "Okay..."

"There's more." I'm pacing now, my voice shaking as I speak. "She was pregnant at the time Sophia, his wife, found out about the affair."

His fingers move to pinch the bridge of his nose. "But...Sophia *is* Celine? Or Celine is Sophia? I'm completely lost."

"The last entry said Celine was coming here to talk to your grandfather, to Simon. To tell him about the baby. Up until now"—I wince—"I thought he'd killed her to protect his secret."

"Up until now?"

"Her family said she died in a car crash with her boss." I twist my lips, contemplating my next words as I work out the only theory that makes sense in my mind. "If that's the case, there's a good chance her casket was closed at the funeral. And your family could pull enough strings...what if they were the ones to identify the body?"

"What are you saying?" He's asking, but I know he understands my implications well enough.

"I'm saying if all of this is true"—I wag my finger at the photo—"and that really is your grandmother... What if the real Celine, what if she and Simon somehow killed his first wife, *the real Sophia*, and Celine took her place?"

"It's impossible," he spits out. "Someone would've known."

"They had kicked her parents out of the house. You've already said the staff is loyal. They'll lie about whatever it takes to protect this family. Who else could've recognized them? Were your great-grandparents still alive?"

"They couldn't have been. Not when my grandparents lived here. The Pond only passes down when the head of the family dies."

I huff out a breath. "Did Sophia have any siblings? I'm assuming Simon's wouldn't have told, even if he did."

"I don't think so. It was just her."

"Then, it makes sense."

"If you say so." He stares down at the picture again. Suddenly, it's as if a light flicks off in him. When he looks up, his expression is grim. "Have you told anyone else about this?"

"Just you." I'm aware of the weight of my words. "Can I trust you?"

"Seems like you already do." He folds the picture up, placing it in the pocket of his shirt.

"What are you doing?"

"Asking you to trust me. Listen, I need you to pack your things, okay? All of it. As quickly as you can."

"What are you talking about?"

"I have to get you out of here."

"What? Why?"

"Because if I don't get you out of here now, you're going to be marrying Lowell in just a few weeks. Is that what you want?"

"What does that have to do with anything right now?"

"It's the only way he gets the house, Austyn. That's why he's pressing for you to marry him now. The Pond is meant to be a family home. If you don't get married, it goes to Fallon."

My heart drops as I recall the conversation Lowell and I had on one of our first nights at The Pond. He'd essentially used Dallas's exact words. *The Pond is meant to be a family home.* He'd talked about stipulations in place to keep him from getting it because he wasn't settled and said multiple times that the house would go to us when we got married. He was telling me the truth without me realizing it. I hadn't been listening closely enough.

Suddenly, another puzzle piece clicks into place for me. I think back to the conversation Fallon and I had in the dress shop this morning, when she was making me doubt Lowell. For just a brief moment, I thought she was being genuine. That she cared about me. Now I realize if we don't get married, she gets the house. That must be what she wants.

It's all been a game.

That's all this family knows how to do.

It's just lies.

Masks.

I flick a glance at Dallas. "Why are you trying to protect me?"

He taps the pocket where the photo rests. "Because apparently the men in my family have a long history of murdering their wives to get their way, and I'm not about to let that happen to you. If Lowell ever finds out you knew about this, he'd kill you."

"What? Why? What does a decades-old murder have to do with me? It's not like I can go to the police with it."

His jaw tightens.

"What aren't you telling me, Dallas? There's something else, isn't there?"

He looks down just as we hear the sounds of Lowell's and Fallon's voices move toward us in the hall. Panic surges through me, but Dallas puts a hand up. "Stay here. Let me handle them." He turns to face the door, then glances over his shoulder, voice low. "Austyn, whatever you do, do not mention any of this to anyone. Promise me?"

I nod. "I promise."

He shuts the door and disappears into the hallway. Not wanting to be left totally in the dark, I press my back to the door, listening carefully.

"What are you doing? Why were you in my room?" Lowell asks.

"She's on the phone with her mom. I was just checking on her. Let's go downstairs and give her a minute."

"I should be the one to check on her."

"Give her a minute, Low," Fallon says. "It's been a long day."

"Well, whose fault is that?" Lowell growls.

"What's that supposed to mean?" Fallon asks.

"*Someone* was the last one here with our missing friend."

"What the hell are you saying?" Dallas demands.

"Not saying anything. Heavily implying it. Where's Emily, Dallas?"

"Oh, you can't be serious!" Fallon cries. "Why would he have anything to do with her leaving?"

"Who says she left?" Lowell barks.

"You're just mad because your little sidepiece left you," Fallon hisses.

The pain of her words hits me square in the chest. So, maybe she did know.

"You have no idea what you're talking about."

"Okay, look, let's take this downstairs. Seriously. She doesn't need this right now." That's Dallas again, and I can hear his footsteps moving away from the door.

At the same time, there are two quick steps toward my door. I hurry backward and swipe my sleeves over my eyes, drying my tears. Just as the door opens, I drop down on the bed.

Lowell stands there, his gaze trailing over me. "Hey. Is everything okay? Dallas said you were talking to your mom."

I nod, hoping I don't seem as terrified as I feel. "I'm okay. We just hung up. You know she calms me down."

"Of course." The worry in his eyes feels sincere. *Why are you such a good liar?* "I'm going to be downstairs if you need anything, okay?"

I nod. "Sure."

"Hey, look..." He checks behind him, where I can see Dallas and Fallon watching from the hallway, then steps inside the room and shuts the door. "I know it's bad timing, but I think we should push the wedding up even sooner. Maybe this weekend? We could do just a small ceremony here. Have your mom, my siblings... Everyone that truly matters." He moves to sit next to me on the bed. "Everything that's happened—with my parents, with Emily and Grayson, and now with Emily leaving—it makes me realize how special what we have is. And how I don't want to waste another minute not being married to you." He reaches for my hands. I hope he can't feel them trembling. "What do you say?"

"I can't even think about that right now, Lowell. Not until we've found Emily and made sure she's okay."

"I understand." He lifts my hand to his lips and presses a kiss on my fingertips. "There's a...another reason I'm bringing this up."

I brace myself. Is he going to tell me about the house? "Being married to me, being a Bass officially, will afford you protections I can't give you right now."

My shoulders tense. I can't help it. "Meaning?"

"Meaning, of everyone here, you were the closest to Emily. God forbid something bad *did* happen to her... Who do you think the police will blame?"

It takes a moment for me to register what he's said. "I'm sorry, are you... Are you *blackmailing* me?"

His hands come up to cradle my cheeks. "No. Of course not. I'm just trying to think ahead. If you're a Bass, I can call in favors with the police. The staff, my siblings... We'll all lie for you."

"I don't need anyone to lie for me. I haven't done anything. I wasn't even here when she disappeared."

"I understand that. I'm just trying to think of the optics. You were her best friend, you guys obviously had some issues lately, and now she's gone. Honey, you know I will do everything I can to protect you, but I can't force the rest of the house to do the same." One corner of his mouth draws in apologetically. "Just think about it, okay?"

I nod, unable to say a word. With that, he kisses my forehead and stands. "I'll be downstairs," he reminds me.

I blink back tears as he leaves the room, never having

felt more afraid. I lean back on the bed, allowing myself a moment to process what's just happened. Rage and fear fight for my attention, my body buzzing with adrenaline.

I'm not sure how long I lie there—several minutes, an hour—contemplating how things got so bad so fast.

My phone buzzes from where it lies on the nightstand. I reach over, expecting a text from Mom. Instead, a lump forms in my throat.

Emily

I can't open the text quickly enough and have to read it twice to understand. Goose bumps line my skin.

> I'm safe, but you aren't. Get out of there, Austyn. Meet me in the cemetery.

CHAPTER THIRTY-FOUR

I carefully plot my route through the house, making sure I won't be caught by Lowell or one of the staff. Once I'm outside, the cold air hits me and I realize I didn't even think to bring a jacket.

It's too late to turn back now.

The sky is dark and cloudy, the grounds only slightly illuminated by the moon. I cross the wet grass quickly, my teeth chattering as I hurry toward the cemetery, checking behind me every few steps.

My body feels on fire with adrenaline and terror, but there's a strange mix of relief in there. Emily is alive. She's okay. As angry as I am with her, it matters to me.

I would never want her to be hurt.

When the cemetery comes into view, I spy the rows of gray headstones, moonlight reflecting on their surface. In the distance, there's the toolshed and, farther back, the actual pond.

A dark figure stands near the two mounds of fresh

dirt, and when the person turns to face me, I realize it isn't Emily.

"Dallas? What are you doing here?"

"Meeting you. I got a text from Emily, too. Said to meet here."

"How do you know I got a text?" I demand.

"She said she wanted to meet us both." He shrugs. "I just assumed she passed that information along."

I check over my shoulder. "Does Lowell know you're out here?"

"Obviously not."

"Well, where is she?"

It's his turn to look behind him. "She should be here any minute. Look, Tex, I'm sorry I couldn't tell you she was okay sooner."

"What do you mean? You knew?"

He runs his tongue over his bottom lip. "Yeah, I knew. I was the one who got her out of there. Just like I'm going to do for you."

"But...why? Why would you have to get her out?"

"Because it wasn't safe for her anymore."

"What are you talking about?"

"I'll let her tell you that." He turns, holding out a hand as another dark figure emerges from the edge of the woods to our left. "'Bout time. I'm freezing my balls off out here."

As she draws nearer, I can just make out the features of her face. I rush toward her without warning, launching myself at her. "Em! Thank God you're okay!"

"Shh!" They both warn me at once.

She eases me off of her. "I'm sorry I didn't have time to say goodbye."

"But why did you leave? What's going on?"

"It's a long, complicated story, and I'm going to explain it as well as I can." She glances at Dallas, who nods. "The first thing you should know is that Grayson and I aren't getting a divorce."

"*You're not?* But I just talked to him—"

"He told me. I'm so sorry we lied to you. We didn't have a choice. I asked him to go along with it while I was here, but we're not getting a divorce and the baby—"

"The baby wasn't a lie, either?" It's why she told me she was sober, I realize. She was laying the groundwork, so I wouldn't be suspicious when she wasn't drinking.

"No, I'm actually pregnant, but the baby is his." She rubs a hand over her flat stomach absentmindedly. "After I told Lowell, something changed. I didn't feel safe anymore. Dallas helped me."

"What do you mean? You told Lowell before me?"

That was why she was in his office, after all.

"I thought it would make him finally tell everyone the truth."

"What truth? And why wasn't it safe?"

"Lowell wasn't going to let me leave. When I went to town, his driver followed me. Closely. If I went for walks outside, the staff were always watching."

"I don't understand."

"They were protecting him," Dallas says. "Lowell. His secret. The Bass secret."

Emily nods, gripping my hands. "I'm a threat to

Lowell, to the Bass family, as long as I'm alive. I've been trying to tell you all week, but I could never get you alone and out of the house. I never knew who was listening. I..."

She sucks in a breath. "When my mom got sick my senior year of high school, she told me a family secret of our own. When my grandmother was eighteen, she fell in love with a man and they had a baby. But my grandmother's parents didn't approve. They wanted her to marry someone else. She was their only child—they hadn't been able to have any more—and she had an obligation to carry on the family legacy. She was forced to marry a man she didn't love but who was from a good family, with quite a bit of money, and who my great-grandfather believed would make a good successor of their business."

"I am so lost. What does any of this have to do with—"

"My grandmother's name was Sophia Bass. She married a man named Simon Parker. Because of my family's lineage, Simon took Sophia's name. And he took my mother, Elizabeth, in as his own child."

"Simon Bass..." I whisper the name, looking up at Dallas, who's studying me with a grim look on his face. "Your grandfather was Simon Bass?"

"Not by blood, no. My grandfather's name was James. He was the man Sophia loved, but her family wouldn't let her be with him." She looks over her shoulder, then continues. "In 1978, they dropped my mother off on her father's doorstep with a note that said Sophia didn't want any ties to her previous life. She only wanted to be with Simon, and she was expecting a new baby."

I try to soak in all she's telling me, but it feels impossible—1978 was the year Celine was meant to have died. The year the real Sophia died. I think back to Celine's journal and the mention of Sophia's baby.

I clean up after her and the baby whenever I'm told...

Why hadn't I thought more of it before? Elizabeth, Emily's mother, had been the baby in the journal, not Lowell's father, John.

"My biological grandfather's family raised my mother —they adopted her and changed her last name—but when she was old enough, they told her the truth about what happened. About who she really was. It was a secret she kept from me until I was old enough, too. And, once I knew, as sick as my mom was, I wanted to meet the rest of my family. The Bass family. To understand why they abandoned us."

She pauses. "When I chose Vanderbilt, a school on the opposite end of the world from where I lived, it was because Lowell Bass had just announced that was where he was going. I thought it was a chance to get to know him in a way with less pressure. I thought if we became friends, it would be easier to tell him the truth about who I was."

"And did you?"

"I did. Right after you guys started dating, I finally worked up the courage because I didn't want to lie to you anymore. I hoped he'd want us to tell you the truth, but I thought he deserved to know first."

"He didn't want you to tell me?"

"Well, I don't think he believed me at first," she says,

"but I was persistent. Finally, he accepted it, but he told me his parents never would. He asked me to give him time to tell them gently. He said it would be hard for them to believe and, if they didn't, they could make my life worse. I just wanted a family."

Her voice cracks. "I trusted him. Believed him. I considered him my family. It wasn't about the money. It truly wasn't. But we *did need* money. I was sending all the money I could back to my mom and dad to help cover her medical bills, but they were drowning. I waited nearly six months before I asked him for help. He offered to send me money monthly, if I kept the deal between us." She's still for a moment. "It was more money than I was making in a year at the time."

"The thirty-five thousand..." I breathe out the words. That's why Lowell showed me the email printed out. It was a fake. He was lying. There was never an attached contract between himself and a cleaner. Why didn't I question him more?

She nods. "He told me you found out about it. Told me I was to lie and deny it if you asked. I'm so sorry, Austyn. I never wanted you to be involved in any of this. I never wanted you to get hurt."

"So, you weren't sleeping together?"

Her head jerks back with shock. "Is that what you thought?"

"You were together all the time, sneaking around, and then I saw the money. And you made that comment about having a crush on him in school."

"We were together all the time because I kept

confronting him and demanding he tell you the truth. Tell everyone the truth. It's why I came here. Why I lied about Grayson. I needed you to invite me here, so I could pressure him. He wasn't answering my calls or texts, and he didn't have his parents around to hide behind as an excuse anymore."

She folds her arms over herself. "Then, when he invited me, I thought he'd had a change of heart. He told me that he would tell everyone, but he needed to find the right way. There was always an excuse with Lowell, but I wanted to believe him because he's my family. The only family I have left. I had no idea I was walking right into his trap."

Her hand rubs over her bicep, trying to warm herself, and it reminds me of how cold I am. The wind is biting. "And I said I was obsessed with him, not that I had a crush on him. Is that what you thought I meant? I wanted to get to know him. I was obsessed with trying to find a way to talk to him, and then you guys became lab partners and it all fell into place. I'm sorry if my words were confusing. I never had a crush on Lowell. I thought we were related."

"Thought?"

It's Dallas's turn to speak. "When we talked earlier, I realized something. If Sophia is actually the woman who died, not Celine, then Celine is the grandmother I knew as Sophia. Which means *Celine and Simon* were our grandparents. Not Sophia and Simon." He pauses. "Which means Emily is the only actual *by-blood* Bass."

"Wait, what?" My hand goes to my chest involuntarily. Can that be true? I hadn't pieced it all together.

Suddenly, I recall Lowell telling me the room we're staying in used to be the primary bedroom, and it hits me. The reason the journal was on the second floor—the family floor—makes sense too. I've been sleeping in the bedroom Celine shared with Simon after Sophia's death. The old owner's suite.

"I had no idea until tonight. When Dallas texted me about Celine, I knew I had to come back. I knew you had to hear all of this in person to believe it." She rubs a hand over her mouth. "When Lowell wouldn't tell his parents the truth, I thought I'd take matters into my own hands. After my dad died too, and I found out I was pregnant, it was just me. I had nothing else to lose. I wanted this baby to grow up with the big family I once had. I thought the worst they would do was send me away."

I shiver, and suddenly I feel Dallas's coat on my shoulders. He doesn't look at me as he places it there, but I pull it over my arms, my teeth chattering.

"I texted Lowell to tell him I couldn't wait any longer, that I was here and going to tell his parents the truth. He ignored me. As scared as I was, I really thought it would all be okay. I wasn't expecting them to welcome me with open arms, exactly, but I thought they'd at least hear me out. Turns out, that may have been the one thing Lowell didn't lie about. John and Alice weren't having it. They accused me of being a gold digger and a liar. They said it was ridiculous. I was all but thrown out, just like Lowell said I would be."

She swallows, looking down. "Two days later, I saw your post on social media. That's how I found out they were dead."

"Did they... I mean, did they know about Celine and Sophia? Could they have known that what you were telling them meant so much more than face value?" I ask.

"We have no way of knowing," Dallas says, "but there's a good chance they knew, yeah. And, if they did, there's a good chance Lowell knows, too. He was always the one they trusted most, the one they would've told. If he worked out what we have after Emily told him the truth about who she was, he would've known the truth of her identity could never come out. Even if he didn't, our family was never going to be okay with this coming out. They only wanted to protect their image—The Bass image—above all else. A secret, abandoned sibling wouldn't do that."

"But then, now that we know, there has to be a way to prove Emily's story. We could go to the police or..."

"The police are on our payroll. Lowell's payroll. And he's not going to help us."

"What about the press, then?"

"It's too dangerous," Dallas says.

"And even if it wasn't, it's my word against theirs. I have no proof other than my mother's story." Emily shakes her head slowly. "All I care about right now is getting you out of here. Making sure you're safe."

"No. That's not right. If this is all true, you are the true heir to all of this. Not Lowell, or Fallon or..." My gaze slides to Dallas. "I'm sorry, but not you either."

"I know." He shrugs. "And I'd love nothing more than to rip this house right out of my brother's smug hands, but Emily's right. We have no proof. The best I can do is get you out of here. At least then, everything passes to Fallon, who might be more willing to listen at some point. I told you, Lowell is in control. He's the nucleus right now. We can't beat him."

Something clicks in my head. "Wait. You're wrong."

"I'm not, trust me—"

"No, you are. I have a way we can prove Emily's story."

"What are you talking about?" Em asks.

I stare back and forth between them both, hope swelling in my chest as the way forward becomes clearer and clearer. "If we could prove that Dallas is related to Celine Mason, it would mean he couldn't be Bass blood, right? That the siblings couldn't be related to the original Bass family."

"Sure, but how would we do that?" Dallas asks.

I grin, cocking my head to the side, chills lining my skin for a whole new reason. "What if I told you I have some of Celine Mason's DNA?"

CHAPTER THIRTY-FIVE

I move through the house alone, tiptoeing up the stairs and to our bedroom. I ease the door open, checking to be sure Lowell isn't in bed.

I have my story ready if I'm caught—I've just been out for a walk, of course.

To my relief, the bed is empty. I cross the room toward the closet, drop to the ground, and stick my hand underneath the dresser where I've hidden the brush with the journal.

My hand scans the space, searching for something. Anything.

Instead, I find nothing. I pull my hand out and press my cheek into the carpet, trying to get a better look.

The journal and hairbrush are gone.

Icy dread seeps into my bones.

No.

"Looking for something?"

His voice is so cold it's nearly unrecognizable.

"Lowell?" I sit back on my knees, pushing to stand. "I didn't hear you come in."

"I saw you sneaking in. Thought I'd better follow to be sure you weren't up to no good." His smile is wicked as his arms fold over his chest. "Guess it's a good thing I did."

"What do you mean?" I ask, trying and failing to steady my voice.

"What are you looking for, Austyn?"

"I… Um…"

"Did you honestly think you could keep anything secret from me for long? In my own house?"

"Lowell, what did you do?" My body goes icy. The brush is our only hope. If it's gone, I'm not sure what chance we will have of ever bringing the truth to light.

"I told you, honey. I'm protecting you. Making sure you stay out of trouble."

"Where did you put the journal?" I try to make him think that's the most important piece to all of this.

"Oh, I wouldn't worry about that. It's somewhere safe."

"How could you do this? How could you not tell me about Emily?"

"Ah, I see you've been talking to your friend, hmm?" His eyes take in the room. "Good to know she's still around here somewhere."

"How can you be this person, Low? I loved you. I trusted you. I was counting on you."

"Yeah, well, I guess it goes both ways, doesn't it? It didn't have to be this way, Austyn. I tried to offer you everything. The world. All of this could've been ours. *Should've* been ours. But you just couldn't leave well enough alone."

"This isn't the world. It's just a house. And none of it is worth hurting someone else."

"I guess that's where we'll have to agree to disagree," he sneers. "I was wrong about you. I thought you had what it took to carry the Bass name, but I was wrong. You're weak, Austyn. Pathetic."

"So let me go. Just let me leave."

He laughs. "Yeah. 'Fraid I can't do that."

"Lowell, you can't keep me here. I'm not your prisoner."

"I have no intention of keeping you here, sweetheart," he says with a sickly sweet voice. "I'm going to get you out of here as fast as I can, trust me on that."

"Let her go, Lowell." The voice shocks us both. When Dallas comes into view, his hands are in his pockets. He seems completely at ease.

Lowell groans. "Oh. I should've known you were involved in this somehow."

"Let her walk out of here and go. No one has to get hurt. Austyn isn't going to say anything."

"Yeah, well, I made that mistake before. Emily was this walking time bomb I thought I could control." He narrows his eyes at me, fists clenched at his sides. "I'm sorry, but I won't make that mistake again."

"I won't let you hurt her."

"I don't need you to *let* me do anything. I could snap my fingers and have four security guards in here in a second. If you think they wouldn't hurt you at my command, kill you even, you're wrong."

Fear flickers in Dallas's eyes, but he presses on. For someone who says they're no good at shutting off their feelings, he's shoving down his fear pretty well. "You don't want to do this. You love Austyn, I know you do."

"There's a fine line between love and hate. Isn't that what they say?" Lowell almost looks like he's enjoying this.

"I won't say anything to anyone," I promise. "Please, Lowell. You have the journal. Just let me go. You wouldn't honestly kill me, would you?"

"I have no choice." It's the first time he's looked even the slightest bit remorseful. "I can't let you go, and I can't trust you to marry me." He drops his head. "But no. I won't be able to kill you myself." When he looks up, he juts his head toward Dallas. "He's going to do it."

"*What?*" we both shout at the same time.

"You heard me," Lowell says. "Take her outside. I don't care how you do it, just get it done." A bit of hope lights in my chest, but he squashes it quickly. "Actually, no. Can't trust you to do it. Wow, this is a first. I guess I'm going with you."

"Like hell. I said I'm not going to let *you* hurt her, and I'm definitely not going to be doing it myself."

"Oh, I think you are."

"And why's that?"

He stares at his brother for a second too long. "Because if you don't, I'm going to tell the police you killed Mom and Dad."

The air is sucked from the room. Dallas's face goes ashen. "What are you talking about?"

Lowell glares at his brother, arms folded, a smug grin on his lips. "You think I don't know it was you? The autopsy showed they had way more than *anything* they would've taken in their system. They weren't stupid, but you were. It was so obvious, but I paid Tom to bury it. I could just as easily have it *un*buried. And given that you were the only person in the house that night—"

"You son of a bitch—"

"Oh." He clicks his tongue three times. "You shouldn't speak of Mom like that."

"They were going to kill her," Dallas says. "I had no choice, and you know it. You warned me she was coming, but you didn't tell me why." His eyes narrow at his brother. "You knew what they'd do."

"I did and, like I said, I tried to protect her from it, but in the end, she was too stubborn for her own good." He shoots a glance at me. "Seems to be a pattern around here."

Some of the color is finally returning to Dallas's cheeks. "I thought you were having an affair—that she'd come to tell them about it. I assumed you were keeping her from talking to Austyn and she thought our family was the next best option. And then, after she left, I heard them talking in the kitchen about having her killed. They were trying to decide who to send after her and how to do it. I just...I just acted. I'd seen enough bad done by this family. I thought I was helping *you*. I thought you cared about her. We don't have to do this. We don't have to be like them, man. To behave the way they did. We can protect people. Do the right thing."

"And then the world would just be sunshine and rainbows, and we could donate all our money to charity and live happily ever after." He guffaws. "Come on, Dallas. I know you couldn't give two shits about living like a Bass, but at least act like you have pride in the name. We didn't get where we are by giving shit away. We didn't get here by bending over and taking it up the ass when anyone causes trouble." He stomps his foot, his voice deepening. "We got here by handling it. Squashing the bugs. Protecting the Bass name above all else. The Bass family above all else."

"Emily is family," I argue, drawing his attention back to me. "She's Bass blood. Even more so than you are."

Lowell looks at me. "Emily is a liar. And a thief. She wants our money. I've been giving her money, more than enough, but she's gotten greedy." His lips hardly move as he says the final words, "She is not my family. And neither are you." He looks at Dallas. "Are you going to handle this or not?"

I'm a *this* now, not a person.

A thing to be handled.

Dallas's eyes shoot between us, back and forth, back and forth. He swallows. Clenches his fist.

"Come on, man. Don't be a fucking pussy. Dad would be so disgusted if he wa—"

"*I'll do it.*" Dallas's strangled voice cuts through his brother's words. When he looks up at me, the man I know has disappeared. In his place is a stranger making full use of those dark eyes. "I'll do it."

Lowell pats him on the back. "Attaboy."

At Lowell's command, Dallas grabs my arm and leads me out of the room. If I struggle, he squeezes me tighter. On our way out the door, we pass two security guards standing at the end of either hall, probably drawn out by my screaming.

Neither of them stops us or asks any questions about the two men leading me out of the house against my will.

"Don't come outside, no matter what you see or hear," Lowell tells them.

They don't meet my eyes. "Yes, sir."

It's the first time I see Dallas's words in action.

Lowell is the nucleus. His rules go. No matter what.

It's why I'm trembling under Dallas's tight grip on my arm, why I'm praying Emily has gotten away quickly enough to send help. Because I don't think I'm safe. As much as I want to believe Dallas has a plan, I'm losing faith in him quickly.

They lead me across the yard, half dragging me, my legs and feet soaking wet from the dew. I search the edge of the trees for a sign of Emily, but she's nowhere to be found. I'm completely and utterly alone.

"Dallas, please," I whisper, keeping my voice low when we manage to get a bit of space between us and Lowell.

"I'm sorry." His words are as painful as his viselike hold on me. "I don't have a choice."

"No chatting up here," Lowell says, jogging to keep

up. "I would hate for anyone to get any sort of ideas."

"I'm taking her to the toolshed," Dallas says, leading us to the door and stopping. He passes me off to Lowell, whose hand slips down to my ass as Dallas disappears inside the wooden shed.

"Pity we didn't have more time to say goodbye." Lowell's brows wiggle in the playful way they've always done to show me he's in the mood to fool around.

Bile rises in my throat. I look away.

"I really do wish there was another way."

I almost believe him.

"There is," I say. "I will marry you, Lowell. I'll marry you and keep your secrets. All of them. I love you. I know you don't want to do this."

He seems to contemplate this for a moment, leaning his head to the side. "No. I'm sorry. I just can't trust you anymore. In another life, I think we would've been great, I really do. But this is the life I've been given. These are the cards we've been dealt." He shrugs, then raises his voice to shout at Dallas. "What's taking so long in there?"

"Sorry, I'm looking for something that'll work."

Lowell shoves me forward into the doorway of the shed. He's boxed me in with his front pressed up against my back. Dallas turns around, his eyes flicking to where Lowell's hand rests at my waist. It's something Lowell doesn't miss.

He presses into me harder. "Want to have some fun with her before you do it?" Lowell snickers. "You haven't exactly been subtle about wanting to have a turn. Now's your chance."

Dallas's grip tightens on the shovel in his hand.

"I'm serious," Lowell says. "Brother to brother. It's the least I can do for you."

My blood runs cold, my throat burning with palpable fear. I can hardly blink. Dallas wouldn't. I don't think he would. Then again, he's currently planning to kill me, so...

His eyes trail the length of my body and come back up. He turns away, continuing to sift through tools.

"Okay, suit yourself. Maybe I'll just do it myself. What do you say, Aus?" Lowell forces his hand inside my pants and underwear without warning, squeezing me hard between my legs. I cry out, bending forward as I feel his hardness against me.

Dallas starts to launch forward but stops himself.

I haven't lost him. Not completely. I see now how hard he's trying to hold it together.

Lowell's hand retreats, and he lifts it to trace a finger across my cheek. I can hear the smirk in his voice. "That's what I thought."

He rams me forward, and I tumble into Dallas, who somehow manages to stop us both from falling. The tools in his hand clatter to the floor.

"I'll give you fifteen minutes," Lowell says. "Should be more than enough." His grin grows. "Actually, let me help you out with a head start. Strip. Both of you."

"What?" Dallas asks.

"Take her clothes off. Then yours."

When he hesitates, Lowell steps forward and grabs the shovel from the floor. "Do it, or I'll have someone else come help you out." His head juts to the house. "Of course, they might get greedy and want a turn, too."

Dallas swallows, his Adam's apple bobbing, and looks at me, both a question and an apology in his eyes.

I tear my shirt over my head without help, then step out of my pants. "You're a psychopath," I spit. It's so cold, I can hardly feel my feet. I throw the clothes at Lowell, tears stinging my cheeks.

He ignores me, heat filling his eyes as he gazes at my exposed body, raking his tongue over his lips. "Come on. Give him the full show, babe. Take it all off."

I can't bear to look at Dallas as I pull my bra over my head, then step out of my underwear too. Lowell tosses them into a pile outside the door. I wrap my arms around myself, shivering so violently I feel like I might get sick.

"You too," Lowell says, gesturing to Dallas.

He undresses just as quickly, passing the clothes over and covering himself with his hands. "What the fuck is your plan?"

"I've already told you... This is my thanks for taking care of our little problem." Lowell throws Dallas's clothes outside and looks us both over with no hint of shame. "Try not to look a gift horse in the mouth, eh, brother? Now then, I'll be right outside, so don't take too long or I'll have to call in some help." He winks, then goes to pull the door shut. "And don't forget...I know what she sounds like when it's real. Don't try any tricks."

When the door shuts, the fear overtakes me. I collapse onto the floor, wrapping my arms around myself in a vain attempt to stay hidden from Dallas. He comes to stand in front of me, his hands trying to cover his own nakedness. He eases down to the ground, his voice low.

"I'm so sorry about this, Austyn."

I swipe a tear, refusing to meet his eyes. "Then how about you don't do it?"

"I wasn't planning to. I was trying to buy us time and figure a way out." He curses under his breath. "I think he figured that out. That's why he's doing this. It's a test."

I lock my jaw, looking at him finally. "And are you going to pass?"

"You know I don't want to hurt you," he says. "I would never hurt you."

"Well, looks can be deceiving," I toss back the words he said to me not so long ago. That feels like another life.

"I don't hear anything!" Lowell slams his fist into the wooden door from the outside. "Should I call Dante? Or maybe Zach?" He laughs to himself. "Maybe both."

Dallas slips his hands under my arms and pulls me to stand. "Listen, if you want to fight him, we can. It's two against one. I was looking for tools, knives, anything sharp, but all I found are shovels and rakes. We can bust out of the door, maybe catch him by surprise and...and...I don't know. I will do whatever you say, but we have to act fast. If he gets more people out here, I might not be able to protect you. I don't think he's bluffing. I've never seen him like this." He reaches out and touches my shoulder gently, his hand shaking. "I'm so sorry I got you involved in this mess. I tried to stop him, I really did, but I should've told you the truth sooner."

"It's not your fault." My teeth are chattering so hard I might chip a tooth.

Dallas leans in. "I know I've teased you, but I swear, I'm not trying anything. I will not hurt you. But you're freezing. Can I… Can I help keep you warm?"

Reluctantly, I nod. His arms come around me, his body pressed to mine, and I'm entirely aware of how naked we are. The proof of it is growing hard against my stomach.

We both ignore it. He buries his face in my neck. "Do you want to try to fight him? I don't see any other way around this."

Our odds of being able to take down Lowell and his entire security team with a few shovels and garden rakes seem low, even if we're able to catch him by surprise. We have to outsmart him somehow. "What was your plan? Before this?"

"I called Fallon," he whispers, his breath warming my skin. He moves his mouth along my collarbone, breathing warm air onto my flesh. As he does, I feel his excitement growing. He's trying his hardest to ignore it. "I called her when I walked into the bedroom earlier. My phone was in my pocket. I needed her to hear the truth for herself. I don't know whose side she'll take in all of this, but I trust her. I don't think she'd want him to kill us. She was always the median between us, not as far removed from the family as me, but not completely drinking the Kool-Aid like him."

He lowers himself slightly, breathing warm air against my chest. My heart thuds in my ears so loud I can hardly focus. I close my eyes as he does it, hating how much I'm enjoying it. He's nearly reached my breasts but isn't crossing that line yet.

He hesitates.

"Tell me if this isn't okay. If you want me to stop."

As terrified as I am, his stopping is the last thing I want. The warmth he's spreading throughout my body is a welcome reprieve from the cold. Slowly, his mouth moves lower. He releases a puff of warm air with each inch he travels. Finally, his mouth moves over my breast, his lips an inch from my skin. His breath comes slower this time. Heat sweeps through my core as something pulls deep in my lower stomach. He switches to the other side and repeats the process.

Something moves over Dallas's shoulder, and I realize Lowell is staring in the window behind us. I suck in a sharp breath, drawing his attention to me. "Dallas, kiss me."

"Wh—" Before he can finish the question, I pull his face upward and press my lips to his, my hands slipping around his neck. He responds with enthusiasm, gripping me around the waist and lifting me up. My back knocks into the wall, legs wrapped around him as our kiss deepens.

To my surprise, every inch of my body is suddenly warm. Bolts of heat pulse through me with his every touch. His tongue explores my mouth, our chattering teeth banging together. He rests one hand on the wall behind us, the other wrapped firmly around my waist to keep me close to him.

It's easy enough to forget we're in this circumstance.

To feel safe with him.

To imagine going out this way. The happiest ending I could hope for at this point. He presses his forehead to mine, our mouths separating, both panting.

This feels real.

Terrifying but real.

Am I losing my mind in this cold?

"I'm not going to pretend I don't want you, Austyn." He shivers. "I've wanted you from the second you walked through that front door. He never deserved you. But... I don't either. And I won't take you. Not here. Not like this."

"He's watching," I warn. "We have to...buy time, right? For Fallon or Emily?" A tear slides down my cheek from the cold.

"I won't force you."

"You're not," I promise, kissing him again. "You gave me a choice to fight, but I don't want to. I don't think we can." His eyes are wide and full of fear. "You aren't forcing me. It's my decision, and it's okay, Dallas." A chill runs through me. "Please just... Please. I'm so cold."

He nods, a question still in his eyes, and I answer it with a kiss. His hand lowers from the wall. I try not to pay attention to Lowell's face in the window. He's turned so he's no longer watching, but he's not going to stop until he's won this sick game.

"Are you sure about this?" Dallas asks. He's holding himself underneath me, and I nod, despite my shivers. The warmth I felt moments ago has disappeared since he stopped kissing me, and I want it back. His hand eases between my legs, cold and shaking, trying to prepare me for what's coming. The whole time, his eyes are locked with mine.

I wonder if I look as terrified as he does.

"Tell me to stop."

I shake my head.

"Tell me to stop."

"No."

"If you don't tell me to stop, Austyn—"

"*Stop.*" Something clicks in my mind.

Dallas sets me on the ground. "What's wrong? Are you okay?"

"I just figured it out." I stare into space, wide-eyed. Suddenly, everything makes sense.

"Figured what out?"

I meet his eyes, trying to make him understand. "You were wrong. This isn't a test, Dallas."

"What do you mean?"

"He *needs* this to happen." In the window, Lowell has turned his face to watch us once again, swiping his hand across the glass to clear the steam his warm breath is causing.

"What are you talking about?"

It all makes sense, and I can see the truth of it in Lowell's eyes, even through the foggy glass. The pain of what he's watching is evident in his expression, but when our eyes meet, it washes away in an instant, replaced with the same icy stare he wore when he shut the door. "He wants us to do this so he won't feel guilty about killing us.

He's watching us. He needs to see it in order to go through with this. If we do this, we're giving him exactly what he wants."

"No. You don't know him like I do, Austyn. I know you think you do, and maybe on some deep, subconscious level, you're right. But the truth is my brother doesn't need to see anything to kill you. Or me, for that matter. He's a Bass before all else. It's ingrained in him. Right now, the two of us are the greatest threats to this family. This company. He can't let us live."

"I don't believe that," I argue.

Lowell raps on the window with his fist, bellowing through the glass. "Enough talking!"

Dallas steps closer to me, keeping his voice soft so Lowell can't hear him. "The only way either of us makes it out of here is if he's dead. Believe me or don't. It really doesn't matter."

I meet Lowell's eyes through the pane of glass. Throughout my stay, I've chosen to believe Dallas more often than not, but right now, I have to believe that what I've shared with Lowell over these past few years has meant something. I have to believe I can appeal to some part of humanity in him.

Stepping around Dallas, I move forward, placing my hands on the icy glass window pane. Fog outlines my fingers within moments.

"I'm not going to do this, Lowell. I won't play your game. I'm not going to sleep with him to make it easier on you."

"Dallas!" Lowell shouts, pressing his face to the window. "I'm two seconds from calling Zach."

I whimper, ice-cold fear settling in my veins, but force myself to go on. "I know you don't want to do this, Lowell. I know you. You don't want to hurt us."

"Austyn, if he calls someone else, I may not be able to stop them." Dallas's whispered warning comes from behind me. "I don't want them to hurt you."

"Lowell, please. Please just look at me. Look me in the eyes. You love me. We're supposed to get married. To have a family. Remember? Remember the night you proposed? All the plans we made? You can't do this, baby. You can't kill me." My voice cracks, and it seems to set something off in him.

His jaw twitches, and for a moment, he just stares at me. Finally, he speaks through gritted teeth, his head banging into the glass. "You really are stubborn, aren't you? This isn't a game, Austyn. I'm not playing with you."

"Of course it isn't. It's our lives, Low. I don't want to die... My mom won't survive this. Please don't do this." Tears fall down my cheeks. Seconds earlier, I'd have thought it impossible, but somehow, they make me even colder. Dallas's body heat warms my back as he moves to stand behind me.

"Come on, Lowell," he begs, his voice low. "Just let us out. Let *her* out. Marry her. Tell everyone she's crazy if you have to, but...not this. Anything but this."

Lowell spins around, storming away from us without a word of warning.

"Where's he going?" I ask Dallas over my shoulder.

"No idea, but come on, now's our chance." Dallas grabs my hand, and we rush for the door. He grabs hold of it.

THUD.

It doesn't open.

Dallas pulls harder, but it doesn't budge.

"What the hell?" Dropping my hand, he places both of his hands on the old metal pull handle and tugs.

Once.

Twice.

"No. No. No." When he looks back at me, his eyes are wide with fear. "He locked us in."

"What? How?" Now it's my turn to pull on the handle. Together, we use all our strength to pry it open, but it's no use. The door isn't moving an inch.

"The shovel," Dallas says, resting his head against the wood. I recall Lowell picking it up as he walked out. "He must've hooked it through the handle so we can't open the door."

"But why?" I move back to the window. "Is he going to leave us to freeze?"

"We'll break out," Dallas says, sizing up the window. It's small, too small for him, but I might make it through somehow and then I could free him. It'll be a tight squeeze, but it's our only option. He grabs a rake from the floor, but I hold a hand out to stop him as something catches my eye.

"Wait. Look. He's coming back."

He lowers the rake, leaning forward to get a better

look. In the distance, I see Lowell coming back. He's carrying something in his hand. Something square-shaped and red.

As the realization sets in, I feel Dallas's hands tighten on my shoulders.

No.

When Dallas pulls me into him, there's nothing remotely passionate or charged about the way he holds me. We're both scared for our lives, with no way out.

"We walked straight into his trap," I whisper, remembering Emily's words.

"He knew I'd never hurt you. Knew this was the only way." Dallas's voice is powerless. It's the sound of someone giving up.

When Lowell appears at the window again, he smiles, holding up the gas can. "Thought you two love-birds could use a little something to help *light the fire*. It'll be a shame for people to find out about your little affair this way. What'll your mom think when she finds out how you two were out here, drunk off your asses, just banging each other's brains out when it somehow caught on fire, Austyn? What a shame you were too wasted to notice the smoke until it was too late." He clicks his tongue. "I've told Mr. Tuttle to quit smoking around this shed."

When he disappears out of view, I smell the gasoline instantly, hearing it slopping against the side of the old wooden shed. The wood is old and dry. It'll go up in seconds. I turn to face Dallas, tears in both our eyes.

The heat hits us in an instant—he's wasted no time for contemplation.

Dallas shakes his head. "I'm so sorry."

His lips lower to mine, and I think, *There are worse ways to go.* I've lost my mind, I know. From the cold and the fear. I kiss him deeper, ready for it to all be over. Hoping Emily has gotten far enough away with our truth. Hoping she'll take care of my mother.

Smoke fills the space, flames lapping at the walls. Our kiss ends as we break away to cough. Reality comes back to me. I'm going to burn up and die in this shed if we don't find a way out. We could break through the window, but a glance outside shows Lowell ready and waiting, a giant grin on his face.

How could I have ever loved such a monster?

How could I not have seen it?

We watch him standing there, his hand raised in a wave. Dallas's fingers link with mine. If this is how it's going to end, Lowell will have to look me in the eye as he takes my life.

He coughs from the outside, the smoke getting to him, too. Through my blurring, tear-filled eyes, I watch his mouth open, blood pouring out.

No. He's not coughing. He's...*dying*?

Dallas and I see it at once, and I shriek, covering my mouth with my hand. Dallas steps forward toward the window as Lowell tumbles onto the grass, his body limp.

Behind him stands our saving grace. Only it's not Emily, as I expected.

From behind her brother's lifeless body, Fallon gapes

at us, the bloody knife still held in her grasp. She snaps out of her stupor in seconds, rushing over to the shed. I hear the scrape of the shovel against the door, telling us we're free, and I have to wonder if this is all a hallucination.

If this is dying.

They always say it's peaceful.

Maybe no one actually knows they've died. Maybe you just go on living.

She thrusts the door open and we rush outside, moving as far from the burning shed as we can before tumbling to the grass in a fit of coughs. If she thinks it's odd that we're naked, she doesn't say as much as she passes us our clothes and checks us over.

"Are you guys okay?"

"'Bout time you got here," Dallas says through a hacking cough.

"Well, you know I like to be fashionably late." She's helping us dress, the mother in her clearly evident, and I remember the phone call.

"You heard everything?" I ask her.

She meets my eyes solemnly, then gives a curt nod. "I came as soon as I could. I kept the phone on the whole way over. I heard everything he said. Everything he did."

"Why didn't you call the police?"

She exchanges a glance with Dallas. "Because they wouldn't have helped. Lowell would've had them on his side. We may protect our own as Bass, but everyone protects Lowell. That's just how it works."

I look over at Lowell's body, blood pouring from the

back of his neck. "What'll we do now?" I should feel something, I think, but I don't.

Once we're both standing and dressed, Fallon walks over to him, bending down and rolling him over. She's solemn as she uses her fingers to force his eyes closed. "We do what we have to. With Lowell gone, I'm the new head of the Bass family. Everyone answers to me." There is no pleasure in her voice as she says it, swiping the blood from the knife off onto the grass. "We need to move him into the toolshed. Just enough to give a reasonable explanation for his death to any police who aren't on our side. He was trapped inside when it caught fire. A terrible accident."

"What about the pond? Would it be easier to take him there? No one would find him," I offer.

"They need a body, Austyn," Dallas says, finally catching his breath. "It's the only way for the control to pass to Fallon."

"Come on," she orders, "we don't have much time."

She's right. The shed is collapsing in the back, smoke filling the sky above us. We move to his body. Dallas takes his shoulders while Fallon and I each get a leg.

I was right earlier. Even now, I can feel it happening somehow. I've shut off the part of my brain that should care about this. The part that knows this is an awful thing to do.

Maybe Lowell killed that part tonight.

Maybe I'm more Bass than I realize.

When it's done, we dart away as a terrifying sound rips through the air.

Creeeeeeak.

I launch myself forward and onto the ground just as the roof caves in.

BANG.

From the grass, I roll over and stare up at the sky. My lungs burn from the smoke and exertion. The heat of the flames spreads through the night sky, warming my cheeks. It's the biggest fire I've ever seen. Ashes and embers soar all around, painting the sky with twinkling orange stars.

We each look at each other. Fallon folds the knife and places it in her pocket. Lowell brought this on himself. It didn't have to be this way.

I can feel each of us thinking it.

"What now?" I ask her, pushing to sit up.

She sits down on the ground next to me. "Now, we wait. When it's burned down completely, we'll have the security team call Tom. It'll get handled. Then you've got some explaining to do." She looks at Dallas expectantly, and something unspoken passes between them.

She heard everything, I realize. *She knows Dallas killed their parents.*

"I'm sorry," Dallas says. "If there was any other choice..." He quickly fills her in on what she's missed, including everything we've discovered about Emily, Celine, and Sophia.

When he's done, Fallon looks at me. "Holy shit. I thought he was just having an affair."

"Me too," I admit.

She's quiet, contemplating. She looks up at the fire,

whispering, "If there was any other choice..."

"I know." I wish I could offer her something else—thanks for saving my life, a promise that everything will be okay—but everything feels so small compared to all that's happened. Finally, she nods. "We need to find the hairbrush. If what you're saying is true, Emily is entitled to Lowell's portion of everything."

It's the last thing I'm expecting her to say.

"I'm not going to just hand it over to her without proof. I'm not a saint, okay? But, if her story is true, she can have what's hers. But I don't care about blood. We are Bass because I say so. Dallas, unpack those god-awful boxes you have all around the house. You can have the house. I didn't want to leave my house, anyway. If Emily wants to share it, you guys can decide that together."

"You'd really do that? Just hand her Lowell's inheritance? The Pond? Everything?" I ask.

Fallon studies me. "I don't need the Bass family money. I made my own with Envo. I never wanted all of this." She waves her hand toward the house. "I mean, the money's great, don't get me wrong. But I've earned plenty on my own. I'm not my brother. Or my parents. I will do whatever it takes to protect my family, my girls, but family ends where lies begin. Lowell was ready to kill for his secrets. My parents were, too. I won't do that." She purses her lips. "Blood doesn't make a family, Austyn. Love does."

I'm speechless, unable to form coherent thoughts. How could two siblings be so totally different?

Once the fire has burned down, we stand and head

for the house. Dallas is quiet as we make our way across the yard, but when I slip my hand in his, silently telling him that somehow we're going to be okay, that I don't blame him or regret what happened, it's as if he releases a sigh of relief he's been holding in all night. The tension melts away, and somehow, despite the fire smoldering behind me and blood drying on Fallon's hands, I actually feel like it's all going to be okay.

"I told you I wanted a sister out of all of this," Fallon says, her voice dry. "Looks like I might just get two."

Dallas squeezes my hand, drawing my attention just up ahead, where Emily stands near the edge of the woods. She's out of breath, panting and crying. When she sees me, I release Dallas's hand and rush toward her, my legs burning as I fly through the wet grass and pull her into a hug that I hope says all I can't put into words just yet.

"I was waiting for Grayson to come pick me up at the end of the driveway when I saw the smoke," she whispers, squeezing me tight. "I was so scared. I thought I was going to lose you." Her hands move around my body, to my face, cheeks, and hair, as if checking to be sure I'm not an illusion.

"It's okay. We're all okay." Looking back at the smoke filling the night sky and around at the family I've gained, I realize it's true.

Lowell is dead.

My life is nothing like it's supposed to be.

And somehow, despite all of that—or maybe because of it—we're all okay.

CHAPTER THIRTY-SIX

NINE MONTHS LATER

My return to The Pond is one I've been both looking forward to and dreading. As the house comes into view for the first time since Lowell's funeral, trepidation settles into my stomach. I tuck my icy hands underneath my thighs, trying to calm my racing heart.

As the car pulls to a stop, I spy Dallas waiting for me on the terrace.

Henry carries my bag inside—just the one. I'm not staying long. Once he's gone into the house, Dallas walks my way. We meet at the edge of the steps, both seemingly at a loss for words.

Over the last nine months, we've stayed in touch. I've stayed in touch with both of the Bass siblings, actually. First, we were dealing with the logistics of Lowell's death and his funeral. Once that was settled and I could go back home, they both called a few times a week to check in. Dallas asked twice if he could visit, but I told him it wasn't a good idea. I needed time. Our conversations were awkward, at first, because of what we've been through together, but we share a loss that very few people can understand.

The kind of loss that is more sweet than bitter, though the bitterness still stings.

"Hi," he says finally. "You...you look good."

"Thanks. You too."

He hesitates, then nods, leaning in for a quick hug. "Your flight okay?" Turning around, he leads us back into the house.

"Yep, it was fine."

When we reach the door, Emily is there to greet us, her daughter swaddled in a pink blanket in her arms.

"Oh!" I cry, stepping forward to reach for my goddaughter. It's the first time I've laid eyes on anything so precious. "Sweet girl." I'm breathless as Emily places her in my arms.

"Hey, friend."

"Hi." I look up at her and Grayson with tears in my eyes. "She's perfect."

"All ten fingers and toes," Grayson says proudly. "And a good little head of hair."

"Like her daddy." Emily tousles his hair.

"Do you want to see her room?" a voice asks from beside me. I hadn't noticed the young girl at first.

"Hello, Harriet," I say. "You've gotten so big."

"Growing like a weed." Fallon appears from the study, her own stomach growing rounder by the day, evidence of my newest little niece who will be making her appearance in just a few short months. She wraps me in a one-arm hug, kissing both cheeks. "Good to see you."

"You, too. You look great."

"Oh, please." She sighs, swiping the back of her hand across her forehead. "I look like I feel—exhausted. You, on the other hand, look stunning. Who made this?" She pulls out the tag on the back of my dress.

"Um...Target?" I laugh.

"Mr. Bass, lunch is ready in the dining room," one of the kitchen staff calls from the doorway.

"Thank you, Ira." Dallas waves.

"I was going to show her Evelyn's room," Harriet says, tugging on the hem of my shirt. "We helped decorate it."

"Right. Yes. I would love to see it." I stare at Emily, not sure I've ever seen her so completely happy. This was all she ever wanted. In my arms, Evelyn coos. I smile down at her in a state of pure bliss.

Harriet takes Dallas's hand, leading the group up the stairs to the second floor. She leads us down the hall and pushes open a door that's been painted pink.

We step into the baby's room and it's every bit as perfect as I imagined, with light-gray walls and a large mural of baby elephants napping on fluffy pink clouds. The curtains are heavy and white, giving the room a dreamy feeling.

"It's beautiful," I say, approaching her crib. I recognize the bedding I gifted Emily at her baby shower. As if she senses we're in her space, Evelyn begins to get restless in my arms.

"She may be hungry," Emily says.

I pass her over to her mother, and Harriet points out into the hall. "Do you want to see my room next?"

"Of course I do."

She takes us on a tour of the rooms, showing off her room and then Harmony's. Both girls now have their own rooms for when they're staying at The Pond, which happens more than Fallon expected from what I've heard. Their doors have also been painted the color of their choosing—blue for Harriet and yellow for Harmony.

Just as we're about to head downstairs for dinner, Dallas reaches for my arm. When I look back at him, he lowers his voice.

"Do you think we could talk for a minute before lunch?"

I nod. "Sure."

He juts his head toward his bedroom and leads me inside.

"The place hasn't changed a bit," I tell him lightly. It hasn't changed, but the people inside it have. Everything feels different now because of what happened here.

Because of what we now know.

After Lowell's death, Fallon had the staff search the entire house from top to bottom to find Celine's hairbrush. When the DNA test came back to prove that the remaining Bass children were the descendants of Celine Mason and not Sophia Bass, Fallon kept to her word of giving Lowell's shares to Emily. The three and their families now share The Pond, with Dallas living here full time and Fallon's family staying most weekends. That was all Emily's idea. She got everything she dreamed of—the money that was rightfully hers, but, more importantly, the family that came with it.

Emily and Grayson moved into The Pond just before Evelyn was born, and she took a position working at Envo with Fallon. Dallas agreed to step in as CEO for Bass Industries under two conditions: he hired a COO to handle the day-to-day operations so he could focus on the things that were important to him, and he completely revamped the company in order to do better than his father had. Though he's assured me multiple times he's no saint or Girl Scout, I've seen this man do more good with his family's money over the past nine months than the Bass family has done in centuries.

In some ways, I think it's Dallas trying to make amends for all the bad things his family has done, all the hurt they've caused, but in reality, it's just who he is.

It's why he wasn't and will never truly be a Bass.

Though I don't know that anyone ever knew it, what Fallon called Dallas's attempts to *find himself* were actually just attempts to accept who he was. For the past several years, without his family's knowledge, he has volunteered for nonprofits across the state, using what he'd learned from his family about business to ensure they were running smoothly.

Lowell was a Bass until the bitter end, but Fallon and Dallas could see where it was leading them. They wanted to distance themselves from it in whatever way they could.

To be honest, I don't know what I would've done if I were in their shoes. Would I have risked everything to go against my family and save a stranger? In Dallas's case, two strangers? I'm not sure.

What I do know is that there is goodness in people, even when you have to look hard to see it.

There was goodness in Lowell, despite what he did. I still remember the way he'd dance with me in the kitchen when I needed cheering up or how he'd once bought every dessert on the menu when I couldn't decide on one. I remember how he took care of me when my dad died and how he held me when I was sick.

Everyone has good and bad inside of them—it's not an original concept, but it's one I've come face-to-face with this year.

One we all have.

"I'm glad you're here," Dallas says, drawing my attention back to him.

"Me too," I tell him. It isn't a lie. Though I was nervous about my return, I feel welcome at The Pond for the first time. Perhaps because I finally know everything. Perhaps because these people, as odd as it is, now feel like family.

"Does it feel weird? Being here?"

"The exact opposite, actually. I thought it would be painful or awkward to come back, but in truth, I'm not sure I ever really left, you know? I needed time to clear my head, but it was never about getting away from any of you. I owe you all my life."

"We know that, but we don't expect anything from

you." He sits down in the chair near the window, and I take a seat across from him. "Have you thought any more about our offer?"

"To come work for you?"

"For Bass Industries, yes. It's not the same company it was."

"I know that." I lean forward, clasping my hands together. "And I'm so proud of all you've done to change it. It's really impressive, Dallas."

"Waiting for a *but*..."

"*But,* as much as I appreciate the offer, I can't work for you. I have the bakery. Besides, it wouldn't feel right."

He nods, his knee bouncing as he stares out the window, then back at me. "It's as much yours as it is ours. You were the one thing my brother got right. Bass Industries never belonged to me, Austyn. And Fallon doesn't want it. Emily's happy working for Envo. I want you to be happy, I think you know that, but we miss you. All of us. I know you don't want to move into The Pond, and I understand that, and if it's too hard for you to be around us, that's understandable, too. But, if it isn't, we'd like to see you more. *I'd* like to see you more."

I study his face, processing what he's said. Once, I thought there would never be a time when I could look at this man and not see Lowell in his features. That I could never hear his voice and not hear the man I was meant to marry. The man whose body I tossed into a fire without a second thought.

Now, though, as I stare at Dallas, I see the man who protected me in that fire. The man who refused to hurt me. The man who gave me a coat when I was cold and an umbrella when it was raining.

In truth, my time away was as much to get over all that had happened as it was to get over my feelings for Dallas. It feels wrong to care about him so much when I was meant to marry his brother.

Just like it felt wrong to be so attracted to him back then.

"I'd like to see you more, too," I hear myself saying.

His smile is bright, but he squashes it down, trying to control himself. "Alright, cool."

"Cool."

I don't know what this means—what it will mean for my bakery or my home or my future—but I know I'm being honest with him and with myself for what feels like the first time in so long.

Life is messy and complicated, and sometimes the things that feel impossible, somehow become your reality.

If you'd asked me a year ago what my future would look like, my answer would've been completely wrong. And yet, that future, the future I envisioned then, now feels cold.

Today, as Dallas stands and takes my hand to lead me down the stairs, I feel warmth in the way he warmed me in the toolshed, a sort of warmth that spreads through your entire core and out to your extremities.

The kind of warmth that comes from love. Belonging. Family.

As we walk into the kitchen and Emily gestures

toward the two seats saved for us, I can't help the grin that grows on my face.

Dallas's thumb rubs over mine before he releases my hand to pull out my chair just as Fallon begins to tell me about her latest doctor's appointment.

This is family.

This is love.

Houses have feelings. For the first time, The Pond feels completely like a home.

DON'T MISS THE NEXT DOMESTIC THRILLER FROM KIERSTEN MODGLIN!

You won't like what you find...

Purchase *Don't Go Down There* today:
https://mybook.to/DontGoDownThere

WOULD YOU RECOMMEND THE FAMILY SECRET?

If you enjoyed this story, please consider leaving me a quick review. It doesn't have to be long—just a few words will do. Who knows? Your review might be the thing that encourages a future reader to take a chance on my work! To leave a review, please visit: https://mybook.to/thefamilysecret

Let everyone know how much you loved *The Family Secret* on Goodreads: https://bit.ly/thefamilysecret

STAY UP TO DATE ON EVERYTHING KMOD!

Thank you so much for reading this story. I'd love to invite you to sign up for my mailing list and text alerts so we can be sure you don't miss my next release.

Sign up for my mailing list here:
kierstenmodglinauthor.com/nlsignup

Sign up for my text alerts here:
kierstenmodglinauthor.com/textalerts

ACKNOWLEDGMENTS

As always, I should start by thanking my amazing husband and sweet little girl—thank you for loving and believing in me. Thank you for celebrating the successes and helping me move on from the failures. I'm so grateful to be able to share this journey with you both. I love you both.

To my wonderful editor, Sarah West—thank you for making each and every book shine. Your knowledge, insight, and advice never fail to make my stories stronger.

To the incredible proofreading team at My Brother's Editor, Rosa and Ellie—thank you for your sharp eye and love for my characters and their stories. There's no one else I'd trust to be my final set of eyes.

To my loyal readers (AKA the #KMod Squad)—thank you for continuing to be my cheerleaders throughout every moment of this beautiful career. Thank you for loving my characters, for trusting me with the most wild ideas, and for always coming back for more. Thank you for every shoutout, recommendation to friends and family, email, review, purchase, and post. Most importantly, thanks for making my wildest dreams come true.

To my book club/gang/besties—Sara, both Erins,

June, Heather, and Dee—thank you for always being the ones I want to discuss my books with first, for never failing to be excited for the next one, and for being the weekly break I need and look forward to. Love you, girls.

To my bestie, Emerald O'Brien—thank you for continuing to be my sounding board every time I change my mind or get a new idea. Thank you for being the first person to read my stories and the one whose wisdom I trust the most. Love you, friend.

To Becca and Lexy—thank you for keeping all things KMod running smoothly. I'm so grateful to know you and consider you both friends.

Last but certainly not least, to you—when I sat down to write this story, I thought of you. I wondered which parts might make you laugh, which scenes would make you angry. I worried over whether the twists would shock you and if you'd enjoy the story I was trying to tell. For so long, I wished for someone to read my stories and now, here you are. Thank you for being here. For being you. Thank you for supporting my art and my dream with this purchase. Whether this was your first Kiersten Modglin novel or your 36th, I hope it was everything you hoped for and nothing like you expected!

ABOUT THE AUTHOR

KIERSTEN MODGLIN is an Amazon Top 10 bestselling author of psychological thrillers and a member of International Thriller Writers, Novelists, Inc., and the Alliance of Independent Authors. Kiersten is a KDP Select All-Star and a recipient of *ThrillerFix*'s Best Psychological Thriller Award, *Suspense Magazine*'s Best Book of 2021 Award, a 2022 Silver Falchion for Best Suspense, and a 2022 Silver Falchion for Best Overall Book of 2021. She grew up in rural western Kentucky and later relocated to Nashville, Tennessee, where she now lives with her husband, daughter, and their two Boston terriers: Cedric and Georgie. Kiersten's work has been translated into multiple languages and readers across the world refer to her as 'The Queen of Twists.' A

Netflix addict, Shonda Rhimes superfan, psychology fanatic, and *indoor* enthusiast, Kiersten enjoys rainy days spent with her nose in a book.

Sign up for Kiersten's newsletter here:
kierstenmodglinauthor.com/nlsignup

Sign up for text alerts from Kiersten here:
kierstenmodglinauthor.com/textalerts

kierstenmodglinauthor.com
www.facebook.com/kierstenmodglinauthor
www.facebook.com/groups/kmodsquad
www.twitter.com/kmodglinauthor
www.instagram.com/kierstenmodglinauthor
www.tiktok.com/@kierstenmodglinauthor
www.goodreads.com/kierstenmodglinauthor
www.bookbub.com/authors/kiersten-modglin
www.amazon.com/author/kierstenmodglin

ALSO BY KIERSTEN MODGLIN

STANDALONE NOVELS

Becoming Mrs. Abbott

The List

The Missing Piece

Playing Jenna

The Beginning After

The Better Choice

The Good Neighbors

The Lucky Ones

I Said Yes

The Mother-in-Law

The Dream Job

The Nanny's Secret

The Liar's Wife

My Husband's Secret

The Perfect Getaway

The Roommate

The Missing

Just Married

Our Little Secret

Widow Falls

Missing Daughter

The Reunion

Tell Me the Truth

The Dinner Guests

If You're Reading This...

A Quiet Retreat

Don't Go Down There

ARRANGEMENT TRILOGY

The Arrangement (Book 1)

The Amendment (Book 2)

The Atonement (Book 3)

THE MESSES SERIES

The Cleaner (The Messes, #1)

The Healer (The Messes, #2)

The Liar (The Messes, #3)

The Prisoner (The Messes, #4)

NOVELLAS

The Long Route: A Lover's Landing Novella

The Stranger in the Woods: A Crimson Falls Novella

Made in United States
Troutdale, OR
05/29/2023

10299941R00164